Blood of the Orc Prince

Lionel Hart

Copyright © 2021 by Lionel Hart

Illustrations by Houda Belgharbi – http://www.houdabelgharbi.com/

Cover design by The Illustrated Page Book Design – https://theillustratedpage.net/design/

All rights reserved.

No portion of this book may be reproduced in any form without written permission from the publisher or author, except as permitted by U.S. copyright law.

Contents

1. Chapter One — 1
2. Chapter Two — 11
3. Chapter Three — 27
4. Chapter Four — 47
5. Chapter Five — 61
6. Chapter Six — 91
7. Chapter Seven — 117
8. Chapter Eight — 135
9. Chapter Nine — 153
10. Chapter Ten — 175
11. Chapter Eleven — 189
12. Chapter Twelve — 203
13. Chapter Thirteen — 211

About the Author — 222

Also By Lionel Hart — 223

Chapter One

"You know what I have to do, right?"

The question came with no prompting as Taegan and Zorvut lounged together in their private study. On opposite ends of the custom chaise lounge that had just been completed for them a few days earlier, Zorvut's much-longer legs stretched out and Taegan's draped over them as he curled into his book. Their comfortable silence had only increased the casual intimacy between them, and Taegan raised a quizzical eyebrow when Zorvut spoke.

"What you have to do?" he repeated, lowering his book to meet his husband's gaze. Though the first few weeks after they had been bonded a second time had been truly blissful, Zorvut had become more withdrawn and pensive as more news of war reached them. Taegan had sensed his worry and fear, though he was sure Zorvut had tried to shield as much of it as he could from the mental link between them. His serious, lost-in-thought expression had become quite familiar to Taegan, though there was a focus to him now that had not been there previously. "No, enlighten me."

"I have to find my biological father. Maybe he can help me figure out how to control this magic," Zorvut answered, and Taegan blinked in surprise. He had not been expecting that response. "If I can learn to use it, fight with it, maybe I could go and subdue my... the warlord. If I can best him, alone... The fighting would come to an end."

Taegan frowned, setting aside his book.

"Traveling seems like one of the most dangerous things you could do right now," he protested. "And besides, how would we even find this man? We know almost nothing about him, not even his name—"

"We do know his name," Zorvut interrupted, shaking his head. "Tomlin Whitmore. That's what my mother said. I've been..." He trailed off, a tinge of guilt leaking through their bond into Taegan's head. "Well, I've been doing some research, you could say. He was a rather well-known bard. He even came through Aefraya once, though it was well before I was born. I've found out a few things."

"Research? How so?" Taegan asked. Mostly, he was surprised Zorvut recalled the name—there was little of that night he remembered clearly.

"Well, bards mainly perform at taverns and inns, right?" he replied. "So I thought I would ask around the inns in town, and it turns out he had performed at a tavern called the Magenta Marigold once. The owner is an older fellow named Castien, and he told me what he knew."

"The Magenta Marigold," Taegan repeated, frowning. "Yes, I know it."

"He said the last rumors he heard were that Tomlin Whitmore retired to a human settlement in the south of Autreth around five years ago, a port town," Zorvut continued. "He didn't know the name, but I looked over some maps, and I'm pretty sure it's a village called Naimere."

"Well, you really did do your research," Taegan mused, glancing away. He was not certain why the discussion left him feeling so unsettled. "I don't know, Zorvut. I understand why you wish to seek him out, but... Traveling is going to be so dangerous right now. I just don't want you to get hurt."

Though affection came through the bond at that, Zorvut let out a bitter laugh.

"Unfortunately, I think the danger will find us regardless, my love," he replied, shaking his head. Taegan grimaced—that was certainly true. Though they had been lying low, the war front seemed to draw ever closer to the castle, and even King Ruven appeared unsettled of late.

Part of Taegan wanted to protest; after all, who could say if this Tomlin Whitmore could—or *would*—help them at all? Yet another part of him was loath to run from a fight. But he tamped down the thought and instead managed a slight smile.

"That's true," he agreed, reaching for his book once more. "Maybe we can talk with my father, see if there's a way to get in contact with this mystery human."

From the way his eyes flicked away, Taegan knew that was not the answer Zorvut had wanted to hear. But he could promise nothing more than that, and ultimately it would be the king's decision if they could leave the castle grounds at all. He suspected Ruven would not want to let them out of his sight, not now.

"Shall I read to you?" he offered, and Zorvut's expression softened from across the lounge.

"I would like that," he replied, and they settled in closer together as Taegan began to read.

"Thank you for waiting for me," King Ruven said brusquely as he strode into the meeting hall, where Taegan and Zorvut were sitting. "And I apologize for my tardiness. My discussion with the captain went longer than I anticipated."

"That's all right," Taegan replied. They had only been waiting in the meeting hall for a few minutes, careful not to disturb the expansive world map laid out across the large table as they settled into their seats. The king had a pile of papers and books in his arms but set them down haphazardly on the map, sitting down across from them. His long, dark hair was tied back in a loose ponytail, and he had obviously just pulled a clean robe over a wrinkled plain undershirt. The bags under his eyes betrayed the stress and lack of sleep he must have been suffering, but he offered them a smile as he sat down all the same.

"I've learned a few things I wanted to discuss with you," the king continued. Taegan glanced over at Zorvut who briefly met his gaze. He could feel a strange mix of hesitance and anticipation coming from the half-orc's end of the bond; he could not say why Zorvut was feeling the way he did, but he himself had been anxious ever since Ruven's manservant had asked them to come speak with the king in the meeting room. Whatever Ruven wanted to talk about privately with them likely was not a positive turn of events.

"Go on," Zorvut said after a moment as the king appeared to collect his thoughts.

"Well," he said, looking down at his clasped hands on the table. "Orc forces continue to draw nearer to the capital. I had hoped that by keeping the both of you out of the public eye, tensions might ease off a bit, but this has not seemed to be the case so far."

"We can fight," Taegan interjected, and both Zorvut and his father's heads swiveled to look at him. A pained expression came over the king's face—Zorvut remained largely expressionless, but a tinge of surprise came through their bond.

"No," Ruven replied sternly. "Taegan, I know you want to fight, but I'm not going to risk that. If the warlord is still pushing for the castle out of some misplaced hostility toward you and Zorvut, letting you get anywhere near them is the last thing I want."

"I've trained all my life to fight," he protested, but from Ruven's expression, he already knew it was a fruitless battle. "To fight, not to run away."

"And I'm sure they've trained to snatch you right off the battlefield and take you straight to the warlord," the king snapped, then seemed to visibly stop himself, closing his eyes and taking in a long, measured breath. Taegan looked away in irritation, but couldn't argue. In the end, his father was the king, and his overprotectiveness had the force of all of Aefraya behind it. When he met Zorvut's gaze, the half-orc gave him a chagrined expression for a brief moment, and he knew Zorvut quietly agreed with his father. That did not come as a surprise.

"But the reason I wanted to talk to you," Ruven continued, a carefully calm expression back on his face, "is that I am considering sending both of you away. I think you will both be safer further from the castle, further from any fighting that might draw near."

Taegan's scowl deepened, but he said nothing. That was not surprising to him either, and neither was Zorvut's slight spike of excitement at the words.

"I agree," Zorvut said quickly. "I've actually been thinking about this, and I have an idea of where we could go."

"Certainly," the king said, unclasping his hands to gesture at Zorvut. "I wanted to ask your opinions, anyway. What is your idea?"

"Well, we were able to learn the name of my biological father, or at least who my mother claimed he is," he explained. "Tomlin Whitmore, a human bard. He retired several years ago, but the rumor is that he moved to a port town in southern Autreth called Naimere. I think that if we can track him down, maybe he can help me... get a hold of all of this." He clenched and unclenched his fist as he said it, looking down wistfully at his palms.

His magical ability had largely been a cause of frustration and little else since their return to Aefraya. When they had explained his sudden gift to the king, he had arranged to have some warlocks from the library work with him, but they had not been able to teach him very much. Whatever source of magic he drew from, it did not seem to be the same as the elven tradition. Even with their guidance, he had not improved at all.

"Hmm," Ruven mused, lifting a hand to his face in thought. "Well, that could be a promising lead. And even if you don't find him, that's far enough away that you should be safe. I don't think anyone would go looking for you there."

"That's true, too," Zorvut agreed, leaning across the table toward the king. "If we leave at night, maybe cut our hair first so we're harder to recognize... I don't expect anybody would think to track us there. No one but us knows of any connection between him and I."

"I don't know, Zorvut," Taegan interrupted—he had not expected his father to agree so easily. "I'm not convinced that this man would be able to help us, or if he even would if he could. It seems like a dangerous journey with no guaranteed benefit."

From across the table, Zorvut's expression faltered, crestfallen. Ruven gave him a strange look as well, though his expression was much less readable than Zorvut's.

"Far less dangerous than going headlong into battle, Taegan," he pointed out, and Taegan glanced away, half embarrassed and half guilty.

"I suppose you're right," he mumbled, sighing. While he still was not convinced, every argument he had against it sounded petty and childish in his head. Zorvut seemed to sense his lingering reluctance, though, and reached across the table to grasp his hand.

"It is dangerous," he said softly, meeting Taegan's gaze. "But we'll be together, so we'll be safe. And I just really think... I truly believe he'll be able to help me somehow. Do you trust me?"

Taegan's hesitance melted away at the earnest expression in Zorvut's golden-yellow eyes. The more time they were spending together, the better he could pick up the nuances of his husband's face—where he had once found the half-orc to be expressionless and hard to read, he could now recognize so many thoughts on his face plain as day. He squeezed Zorvut's fingers and nodded, pressing his lips into a tight smile.

"Of course I trust you," he replied, and took a deep breath before looking back over at the king. "And you think this is a good plan, Father? Better than whatever you had in mind?"

"To be honest, I didn't have anything specific in mind yet," Ruven said. "I wanted to see what the two of you thought first, and just as I suspected, you already had an idea. And, Taegan, if you are still unsure about traveling so far, perhaps you can remain behind and we can send Zorvut off with an escort. I'm sure one of the land barons would offer you a comfortable place to stay out of the way of everything."

Taegan balked at that, giving the king an incredulous expression. "Certainly not!" he exclaimed, shaking his head. Zorvut chuckled at his theatrics, but he felt the same immediate rejection of the idea coming from the bond as well. "No, whatever we decide on, we do together."

"Good," Ruven replied with an amused grin. "That's what I wanted to hear. Well, I believe Zorvut's idea of disguising yourselves when you leave would have merit. I think haircuts might be in order for the both of you. Zorvut, can you grow a beard?"

The half-orc grimaced at that, but nodded. "It's not flattering, but maybe that's for the best."

Chapter Two

They were on the road within a week, each with shorter hair and plainer clothes, and a patchy dark scruff coming in along Zorvut's chin and jaws. Taegan had been loath to cut his hair, and could only bear to have it cut to his shoulders, while Zorvut's long black hair was now just a short tuft on the top of his skull. He was allowing the sides he normally kept shaved to the skin to grow out a bit as well, giving his head a much rounder shape. He looked almost nothing like the man Taegan married, either the first or second time, so it had been a shock when he had returned from the castle barber shorn like a sheep. That had been even more saddening than his own haircut.

"It's just hair," Zorvut teased as Taegan fought against tears and ran his hands through the short, wiry black strands where there had once been long, luxurious locks. "I like how yours turned out. It accentuates your jawline."

"Don't try to flatter me," Taegan replied, trying to tease back, but he knew the sadness he felt was certainly loud and clear through the bond.

This would also be the first journey on his new horse, another bitter milestone. The mare was a tall red dun with a white line running from her forehead down between her eyes. Her summer coat was a lighter tan shade, while her mane was a deeper reddish hue, and a single braid ran down it. Ember, a fitting name, was much more spirited and lively than his gentle Moonlight had been, but she rode well and got along with Graksh't. Hopefully, she would do just as well on their long trek.

They left less than an hour before the sun set. King Ruven saw them off at the back gate, which let out at the less-traveled trail that made a wide loop around the walls of the city before reconnecting with the main road further southeast. They had planned out their full route, and would break off from the major road once they got further from the capital and closer into contested lands that might have orc scouting parties; still, it was best if no one witnessed them leaving. The fewer people that knew they were not within the safety of the castle walls, the better.

Ruven fussed with Taegan's traveling cloak for a long moment, not meeting his gaze, before finally letting out a deep sigh.

"My son," he said quietly, gripping Taegan's shoulders. "You must exercise every caution. These are dangerous times."

"Yes, I know," Taegan agreed. "I will."

"Remember, if you must write, have it sent to Castien at the Magenta Marigold. He knows to pass the message along to me. But only try to keep it to one, maybe two letters, one when you've arrived and another when you're on the way back. And only if it's safe."

"I know," Taegan repeated, and patted his father's forearm nervously. As anxious as he was about the journey, knowing his father was also afraid made it somehow harder to bear. "I promise we'll return safely. The both of us."

"Yes, we will," Zorvut agreed, nodding at the king. He had already mounted his horse, and was standing a few paces away, waiting for their goodbye to be over.

"Good," Ruven replied, bowing his head. His mouth twitched as if he meant to say more, but couldn't seem to make the words come. He adjusted Taegan's cloak once more, then took a long step aside with a tenuously neutral expression on his face. "Goodbye, my son."

"Goodbye, Father," Taegan echoed, forcing a slight smile as he turned to Ember. "We'll be back before you know it."

The king did not reply, only nodded his head before turning to go. Even though it had been his idea to send them away, he seemed to be having a much more difficult time of it than Taegan would have expected. It would be the first time they'd be apart for longer than a few weeks. It would be the first time Taegan had ever left Aefraya. Both thoughts filled him with apprehension.

"He's your father, of course he's going to worry," Zorvut said wryly as Taegan mounted his own horse. "He would worry even if we weren't at war."

"You're right," Taegan admitted with a sigh. As nervous as he was, he couldn't feel any such emotions from Zorvut, only an eager determination. "It's just... strange, to see him so nervous. It's rare to see him emotional at all, I suppose."

A soft protectiveness welled up from the bond, and he managed a smile at Zorvut, who was still watching him closely. The horses started off at a peaceful walk; it would be a long journey.

After an hour, it had become too dark to see, and Zorvut pulled out a torch. Taegan watched him hold it to his hand for a moment, visibly concentrating—then a flicker of flame appeared between his fingers and caught the torch, illuminating their path, and Zorvut looked back over at him with a satisfied grin.

"Soon, I'll be able to do a lot more," he said, and Taegan couldn't help but grin back. The hope in Zorvut's face would have been apparent even without the echo of it in the bond, and he too, hoped that would prove true.

They traveled well past midnight that first day, sleeping late into the morning before breaking camp and setting out once again. Traveling straight through the night would be difficult, especially when they neared the more mountainous terrain that served as a natural border between Aefraya and Autreth, but staying off the main route during the peak morning hours for now would hopefully help them avoid most of the traffic, the greatest risk of danger.

But during the day, they passed very few others on the road, a handful of merchants but not much else. With times being what they were, Taegan wasn't surprised—who would willingly be on the road with the threat of an orc invasion constantly overhead? His heart would pound and leap up into his throat the first few instances they spotted the form of another traveler drawing near; although they would often look curiously between him and Zorvut as they approached, it didn't seem as though anybody recognized them outright, and the interest seemed to fade away as soon as they were out of sight. Still, he wondered if anyone quietly made a note of seeing them and might make a connection—or a lucky guess.

"Maybe it would be best if we were a little split up," Zorvut suggested, sensing his nervousness.

"Perhaps," Taegan replied hesitantly, but shook his head after a moment. "No, I don't want to go too far from you. It might be more dangerous for you to be seen alone." Zorvut seemed to consider it, then sighed.

"You're probably right," he conceded, glancing away. "An orc traveling around by himself might draw more attention than the two of us together. I don't think anyone's likely to tell the difference between an orc and a half-orc on sight, either."

"Maybe we should wait until we've entered Autreth," Taegan said. "We'll be less of a spectacle there."

"Well, it won't be as risky to be seen together there, of course."

"Fair," Taegan agreed. "I was also thinking... Maybe we could see how far apart we can get while still being connected. It might come in useful to be apart but still able to communicate."

"Hmm," Zorvut replied, clearly surprised at the prospect. "I've never thought of that. But you're right, that could be helpful. I still think we should stay close for now, just to be safe, but like you said. Once we get into Autreth, we'll try it out."

"Nothing too extreme at first," Taegan interjected quickly, and Zorvut chuckled. "Just... to test the limits."

"Of course," Zorvut replied, and he smiled faintly at Taegan. "I love you."

Taegan felt himself blush, not expecting the affection. "I love you, too," he stammered, glancing away. "Of course I do. What brought that on?"

"Nothing," he said with a shrug, grinned as he turned to look out toward the road again. "Do I need a reason?"

He paused, then added more quietly, "Pull your hood up. A caravan's coming up the road."

Taegan silently obliged, pulling the hood of his rough brown cloak up over his head. The color was not at all flattering, but he supposed that was the point of it—though he would have appreciated it if the garment were only ugly, not both ugly *and* scratchy. Ahead of him, Zorvut lifted the cowl of his cloak higher up to cover the lower half of his face. If his tusks were not visible, from a distance—and if it were later in the day with less light—he could possibly pass as a very tall, strong human, maybe made to seem taller from the size of his horse.

The caravan came into view as Taegan rounded the corner. It was small, just two horse-drawn carts, each with a driver and three figures walking alongside. From the distance they were at, it was hard to tell if they were elves, but the carts looked plain and unassuming, one with a crate of apples peeking through the tarp that covered the back. By the time they were close enough that Taegan could tell they were three elves, a half-elf, and a human, he could see each of them staring directly at Zorvut, his impressive height far more eye-catching than his own average stature.

Taegan gave them a polite nod of greeting as they passed on the road, which they returned. One elf that was walking alongside the carts swiveled his head to watch Zorvut as they passed and did not turn his attention back to the road in front of him until Taegan glanced back at the group surreptitiously. He could just make out the farm logo emblazoned on one of the carts, painted in green lettering. He did not recognize the name, though it seemed safe to assume that they were farmers or merchants heading into the city to sell their wares. Most of the land on this side of the capital was still used for farming.

Their last conversation still fresh in his thoughts, he imagined one of the apples he had seen peeking out from the cart. As he thought about it, he tried to push the thought toward the point in the back of his head where his bond with Zorvut was. *Apple*, he thought toward the bond, concentrating as hard as he could while still keeping an eye on the road ahead and focusing on the reins in his hands. *Apple. Apple.*

Confusion started to trickle from the bond, and he glanced up to find Zorvut looking back at him with a strange expression.

"Are you thinking about apples?" he asked incredulously, and Taegan stifled a laugh.

"It worked," he said, nodding. "I was just thinking about what we were talking about with the bond, and... I don't know. I thought I'd experiment."

Zorvut chuckled, stopping briefly so they could travel side by side. "That was very strange," he said, shaking his head with a wry grin. "It was faint, like... like trying to remember a dream about an apple. But I definitely felt it."

"Well, at least we'll have something to pass the time now," Taegan replied with a grin of his own. He eyed Zorvut up and down, his eyes lingering at the half-orc's groin. "Well, two things, maybe."

Zorvut laughed again. "You're insatiable," he said, but the heat he felt through the bond was unmistakable. It would be several hours before they made camp for the night, but Taegan made a mental note to be sure they were well off the trail when they did.

Soon, they broke off from the main road and made their way up a winding mountain passage that would let out on the other side of the border into Autreth. It was slow going over the old, rarely used road, with the path often narrowing suddenly or curving into steep switchbacks. Graksh't in particular had a hard time with the steeper paths, and Zorvut would often have to dismount and lead the horse if the trail became too narrow.

Here, it was far more desolate and remote, and they did not see anyone traveling the same road the entire time they traversed the mountain. On the second night, they camped alongside the trail on a relatively flat stretch of land, and roasted a rabbit Taegan had shot through some underbrush earlier in the afternoon.

"So what is it that you're hoping this Tomlin Whitmore can teach you?" Taegan asked as they sat around the fire after their meal. Zorvut glanced at him with a raised eyebrow, the light of the fire flickering across his face.

"I told you, to teach me to use magic," he replied.

"Well, yes, but what exactly are you expecting to learn? If he's a bard, do you think he could show you anything helpful for fighting?" Taegan asked. Zorvut paused, seeming to ponder the question for a long moment before answering.

"It would be great if I could learn something I could apply to combat," he said slowly, considering his words.

"But if I could even understand how to control it better—how to conjure more than just a handful of fire—just that would help. And maybe I could figure out more on my own from there. As it is, I don't even have the basics down, really. So anything beyond that would be a step up."

"And if he can't teach you? Or refuses to?" Taegan pressed, leaning closer to the half-orc.

"Then I have met the man who is actually my father, if nothing else," Zorvut replied, sighing. A tinge of exasperation came through the bond as he said it. "I understand you have your qualms about this, and in all honesty, they are justified. But I need to know for sure."

"I know," Taegan said, more quietly this time. "I mean, we've already come this far. I'm not going to make us turn back now."

Zorvut gave him a chagrined smile. "I know," he agreed, reaching over to pat his knee. "Thank you for supporting me in this. I know it was not your first choice."

"You are my husband," Taegan replied. "I made a vow to support you, and I intend to keep it."

An intimate, warm fondness bubbled up between them as he said it, and Zorvut pulled him closer, leaving his arm around Taegan, though he said nothing in response. Taegan leaned into him and looked up at the stars, searching for familiar constellations.

"We should try that thing you mentioned," Zorvut said after a few moments of comfortable silence. "Testing the limits of the bond, how far it can go. I think this is a safer place for it."

"Tomorrow," Taegan replied, pressing his head against Zorvut's shoulder. "I want to be near you for tonight."

"Tomorrow, then," Zorvut agreed, and kissed him.

Being intimate on the road had proven to be somewhat messier than Taegan liked, but he could not help the desire that stirred in him at the affection. He could feel Zorvut grin against him, feeling his arousal, and pulled away.

"I told you you're insatiable," he murmured, pulling Taegan into his lap before he could protest.

"It's not my fault," Taegan protested, grinding against the thick bulge of the half-orc's erection. "*You're* irresistible." He whined as Zorvut's hands slipped under his shirt, brushing across his abs and nipples as he yanked the garment off of him. "And you're not exactly complaining."

"No, not exactly," he replied, his voice a familiar low rumble that betrayed his own desire. "Take those off."

Taegan quickly obliged, shifting his weight to pull off his breeches, freeing his cock that was already rock-hard. Zorvut wrapped his hand around it, making him hiss at the sudden friction.

"No," he whimpered, even as his eyelids fluttered in pleasure. "No, I want..."

"Tell me what you want," Zorvut growled, still stroking him.

"I want you to fuck me," he said. His hands reached for Zorvut's pants, fumbling with the laces fruitlessly. "I need you inside me."

"Stand up," Zorvut said gruffly, his voice vibrating through his chest. Taegan nodded, standing up to watch as Zorvut unlaced his breeches and peeled them off. His huge, beautiful cock sprang free, the tip brushing against the half-orc's abs and leaving a glistening smear of precome in its path. "Turn around."

Taegan hesitated at that, then obeyed. Immediately he felt Zorvut's hands grasp him by the waist, pulling him back onto his lap, but this time with his back pressed against Zorvut's chest. One arm wrapped around him, holding him tightly, and the other was under him, spreading his ass apart and pressing a finger into his wet hole. He groaned, trying to press down and fill himself with it, but Zorvut held him firmly in place, slowly and gently working him open despite his protests for more.

"Always so eager to get right to it," he murmured as Taegan wriggled against him. "There is pleasure in this, too, you know."

"I know," Taegan said, biting his lip. "Of course I know. I just... I want to..." He trailed off, unable to put into words the way that Zorvut stretched and filled him to bursting utterly consumed him. There was no sensation like it and was now inextricably linked with any feeling of desire he had. Zorvut made a soft, rumbling sound of recognition, sensing his wordless feelings, though Taegan had no idea how much of it he understood.

"My spoiled little prince," he murmured, spreading him open with two fingers. "I think you're ready for me now."

Taegan nodded eagerly as Zorvut's fingers pulled out of him, quickly replaced by the pressure of the head of his cock against his entrance. The half-orc's grip around his waist had loosened, and slowly Taegan lowered himself onto his cock, hissing first at the familiar burn as it stretched him wide. The sound steadily became a groan as he took in more and more, until finally he was sitting again in Zorvut's lap, filled to the brim with his huge cock. At this angle, as he glanced down, he could just see a hint of a bulge where it pressed against his belly from inside.

But his thoughts were quickly interrupted as Zorvut's hands spread his legs apart wider, and one came up to his chest and pulled him closer, so his back was flush against Zorvut's chest and his whole body on display. Though there was no one around to witness them, it somehow felt extremely lewd, his legs splayed wide apart and his arms lifting to wrap around Zorvut's neck—the thought only made him harder.

"Fuck," he moaned as Zorvut began to move, sliding in and out of him in slow, careful movements. "You feel so good." He felt more than heard Zorvut groan in agreement, pleasure arcing between their bond in an exponential feedback loop. For a long moment he moved at the same leisurely pace, the wet, slick sounds of their movement only occasionally broken by a soft gasp or panting breath. Every nerve in Taegan's body felt warm with pleasure, but he desperately wanted—*needed*—more, needed the intense pressure welling up inside him.

"Harder," he managed to whimper, and he felt Zorvut nod his head. Then one of his hands, so much bigger than Taegan's, pulled his face up to kiss him. Their tongues teased against each other, then Taegan gasped sharply as Zorvut obliged with his request, fucking him faster. He whimpered as Zorvut kissed him harder, his free hand moving to stroke his cock. Taegan clutched desperately at Zorvut's neck as he bounced up and down on his cock, the hot pleasure shooting through him rendering him unable to do anything but hang on for the ride.

He didn't last long, between the hand stroking him and Zorvut's cock filling him completely. He moaned against Zorvut's mouth as he came, his body clenching hard around the huge cock as he shot streams of come onto his abs and chest. Zorvut growled in his ear as his climax flooded the bond, giving him only a few more rough thrusts before Taegan could feel warm, viscious liquid filling his belly, the half-orc groaning in satisfaction.

They remained joined for a moment afterward, each of them panting to catch their breath, Zorvut's hands trailing in idle, comforting circles along Taegan's arms and shoulders. Finally, Taegan managed to find his legs and gingerly lifted himself off, biting back a moan at the sensation of the cock slipping out of his overstimulated hole. It seemed to go on for miles, especially when it was followed by the thick gush of come spilling out of him in a steady stream for several seconds.

"Let me help," Zorvut said, standing up to reach for his pack, from which he pulled out a towel.

"It's futile," Taegan chuckled, though he started to wipe himself off with it. "I don't think I'll be clean again until we find somewhere with a hot bath."

Chapter Three

After a few more days of travel, they reached the border between Aefraya and Autreth. On this mountain trail there was no marker or indication of the crossing, but when they consulted their map in the evening, they decided they must have descended the mountain enough that they had to be in Autreth by now, and should be able to reconnect with the main road the next morning. They would likely even find a roadside inn to stop at by the following evening.

"Hopefully they have a good bath," Zorvut teased, and Taegan chuckled. Though he said it in jest, he hoped a hot bath would be possible—the dirt and grime of the road, among other things, was by far the least pleasant part of the trip so far. He could not recall ever having smelled so much in his life.

"Well, now that we're out of Aefraya," he said. "Should we try testing the bond like we talked about?"

"All right," Zorvut agreed, then seemed to hesitate. "Let's just be careful. We're not that far from the border. Why don't I go on ahead?"

Part of him bristled at that—he was perfectly capable of protecting himself—but the rational part of him knew that Zorvut's request was reasonable, and it was always a good idea to remain cautious, especially in a place neither of them had been before. So he nodded, pulling back on Ember's reins, so she slowed to a stop.

"Go on," he said, gesturing with one hand. "I'll wait for a minute, then I'll follow slowly."

"Stay focused on me," Zorvut said, and he kicked his heels into Graksh't's sides, sending them galloping down the road.

Taegan closed his eyes and took in a slow breath, focusing on the pinpoint of heat in the back of his head near the base of his skull where their bond lived. He could feel Zorvut projecting something toward him—a sense of uncertainty, curiosity, trying something new. Ember shifted nervously under him, unsure why they remained behind, but he tried to keep as much of his attention on the bond as he could muster even as he opened his eyes and nudged her forward at a leisurely walk.

They trotted along for a few minutes until the connection suddenly vanished. There was no pain or discomfort—just a sudden silence where there had once been sound. It was a strange sensation after having focused so intently on the bond, as if he had been staring out a window only to have a curtain instantly, unexpectedly dropped over it. Taegan pulled back on the reins, waiting for a moment to see if it would return. Just when he started stepping forward once more, he felt the bond snap back into place, a sense of *returning* coming through it. It had reappeared as quickly as it had vanished. He had suspected it might feel like a candle flickering back to life, but it had not been like that at all—it simply was, then was not, and was again.

Zorvut appeared on the road after a moment, slowing to a trot as he approached.

"It was just like you said," he called out as he came within earshot. "I had gone about a mile before it cut off. Are you hurt at all?"

"No, not at all," Taegan replied, startled. "Why? Are you?"

"No, no," he laughed, shaking his head. "I suppose I was just worried it would be uncomfortable, after... well, after everything. That's good to know." They walked alongside each other for a moment; Zorvut was clearly thinking, and Taegan glanced over at him curiously. "I'm wondering if there's a way to increase the distance we can sense each other from? Like stretching a muscle."

"I don't know," Taegan said, the question taking him by surprise. "I've never thought of it before. Maybe? Why?"

A strange sort of hesitance and worry bubbled through the bond for a moment before Zorvut seemed to pull his emotions back, though a frown was visible on his face.

"It could come in handy if something bad were to happen," he said simply. Taegan mirrored his frown, his brows furrowing.

"What does that mean?" he pressed, and Zorvut glanced away.

"If we get separated for any reason," he said. "Maybe I'm overthinking, Taegan. But we have few allies, and many who would like to do us harm."

"Is that what all this was about?" Taegan asked, tilting his head. Zorvut only glanced away, but his silence was answer enough. A cold tendril of fear crept up his belly at that—the half-orc had seemed so fearless, but if he had truly been so worried this whole time... The thought of it made him balk. "Zorvut, if you were so concerned, we could have just stayed in Aefraya, where we'd be safe."

"No," Zorvut replied firmly, shaking his head. "I wanted to do this. I *need* to do this. And there's no guarantee we would have been safe there, either. It's just best to have a plan for the worst, I think."

Taegan did not respond, unsure of what to say. Zorvut wasn't *wrong*, of course, but it was unsettling all the same to hear him discussing it so casually. He thought of how comfortable—and *clean*—he could be at home right at that moment, and something in his chest ached.

Zorvut glanced back over at him with a softer expression, clearly sensing his upheaval. "Have you ever been this far from the castle before?" he asked. Wordlessly, Taegan shook his head—it seemed silly, but the question only made his heart squeeze painfully again. Zorvut pulled back on the reins so he stopped, and Taegan did the same so they stood side by side on the road. Gingerly, Zorvut reached out and clasped his hand.

"I'm sorry I made you worry," he said. "I know you're homesick. Hopefully we'll be heading back before you know it."

Taegan blinked—he had not recognized it until Zorvut said it, but he *was* homesick. The realization felt embarrassing, and somehow sad. He glanced away, pressing a hand to his eyes that suddenly burned with tears.

"Taegan," he heard Zorvut say softly, touching his shoulder.

"Sorry," he blurted out, looking back up at his husband. He could still feel his eyes stinging, but he kept them dry through sheer force of will. He wouldn't cry over something so trivial. "I just... I really think I'll feel better after a bath."

Zorvut paused, surprised, then let out a soft sigh with a knowing half-smile and released his shoulder.

"Let's get a move on, then. Maybe we can reach the inn sooner tomorrow if we're fast."

With some effort, they made decent time and the little roadside inn came into view well before sunset the next day. It was a simple, two-story wood building with a stable on the opposite side of the trail, and the trees had been cleared out around them but became more dense in the distance. The sight of it made Taegan feel equal parts relieved and nervous—grateful to be off the road even for just one night, but anxious that they might be recognized or worse, now that they would be in the presence of others.

"Don't be afraid," Zorvut said in a quiet murmur as they approached the stables. Taegan nodded, but before he could respond a stable boy came jogging up to them, a human probably no older than fourteen. His eyes were wide as he approached, but Taegan could see his gaze was locked on Graksh't, clearly in awe of his size.

"Sirs," he said, pulling his attention away from the massive stallion to nod politely at each of them. "I can take your horses from here."

"Certainly," Taegan said, dismounting and handing the boy Ember's reins. Zorvut glanced between the boy and Graksh't, then said,

"I'll help. He can be nervous around strangers." The boy shrank back from the horse at that, but nodded and waved for Zorvut to follow him to the stable. The half-orc peered back at Taegan; the thought of *wait* rang through his head clear as day, and he bowed his head in agreement.

From what he could see, the inn seemed quiet, but not totally empty. There were a few other sets of hoof prints to and from the stable that seemed relatively fresh, and he could faintly hear music coming from the inn across the road. That was probably the best he could hope for, he told himself—better than a bustling, busy tavern where anyone could recognize them, but some place totally abandoned could have its own downsides. Better to just be two of a handful of faces rather than the only patrons for the day, guaranteed to stick in the innkeeper's memory.

Zorvut rejoined him shortly, stretching his arms as he strode out from the stable. He met Taegan's gaze and flashed him a quick smile, and they walked together to the doors of the inn. The entrance led to an open dining area with a long bar on the opposite wall with two humans, a man and a woman, working behind it. The woman called out to them cheerfully in greeting as they entered. In the far corner to their left, a dwarf perched on a stool, strumming a lute and singing. He looked to be older, with gray hair and a long, salt-and-pepper beard, but wore a coat that was an ostentatious shade of purple. Taegan tried not to stare—he had never seen a dwarf in the flesh before, as they were quite insular and rarely left their homeland of Robruolor far across the eastern seas. But the dwarf paid them no mind, continuing his song. Other than the musician, Taegan saw only one patron in the dining hall at the moment, a human man dressed in leathers and furs who glanced up at them as they entered, then back down at his table where he appeared to be fletching an arrow.

"Welcome, welcome," the woman from behind the bar called out to them. "Rooms for the evening?"

"Just one room, please," Taegan said as they approached, and the woman nodded, pulling up a ledger and a charcoal pencil.

"One room, two beds, then," she said, glancing through the parchment. Taegan glanced over his shoulder at Zorvut, who shrugged nonchalantly. But the trickle of amusement that came through their bond made him suppress a grin.

"Separate beds," he agreed, hoping his bemused tone was not as obvious to the woman as it seemed to him. "And if you have baths available..."

"Of course!" the woman agreed. "Let me just get your names, and I can have a bath drawn for you now if you'd like."

Taegan blinked. How had they not decided on fake names yet? He could feel a spike of anxiety from Zorvut as well, so he forced himself to open his mouth before their sudden silence became suspicious.

"You can put it under the name Alain," he blurted.

"Very well then, Alain," the woman said, and Taegan regretted the choice immediately, the sound of his father's name sending a dull ache through him like prodding a scar. "I'll go have a bath prepared for you now. You're in room eleven, which is upstairs at the end of the hall on the left. The bathrooms are down here on the first floor. I'll come get you when the bath is ready. Anything you need in the meantime, you can just ask my husband here, Danyel. I'm Nessie, if you need me."

"Thank you, Nessie," Taegan said, giving a terse nod. She grinned back and left the bar, leaving behind her husband, who gave them a polite acknowledgment although his expression was much more bored. He could feel Zorvut watching him, but kept his gaze on the human barkeeper.

"Something to drink?" the man, Danyel, asked, noticing his stare.

"Wine for me, whatever is your best," he replied, then gestured toward Zorvut. "And whatever he'd like as well."

Zorvut paused, then came to Taegan's side to sit next to him. "Just ale for me, please," he replied, and the man nodded, bending down to retrieve the bottles. He felt Zorvut's hand underneath the bar gently squeeze his knee, and he gave the hand a few soft pats before lifting both his elbows to rest on the bar top. After a moment, Zorvut's hand pulled away as well.

Danyel presented them with their drinks, and Taegan gave him a few coins, waving away the change. He took a sip of the wine, and nearly spat it out immediately with how sour it was. If this was truly their finest option, he couldn't even imagine their common drink. It had no depth of flavor and may as well have been vinegar; he forced himself to swallow, coughing and clearing his throat afterward, before primly pushing the goblet across the bar. Next to him, Zorvut was stifling a chuckle.

"Not what you're used to?" he murmured, grinning down at him. Taegan huffed, glancing away.

"No, it's not," he said. His cheeks burned with embarrassment, but the other patrons seemed to pay them no mind, and the human simply shrugged and took the goblet away, replacing it with a cup of cool water. Taegan took a hesitant sip from that; it tasted like common well water, but it would do.

Zorvut downed his own ale effortlessly, then placed a hand on Taegan's shoulder.

"I'll go to our room and get everything unpacked," he said, and Taegan nodded. "Enjoy your bath."

"Thank you," he replied, and managed a slight smile as the half-orc took the bag that was slung around his shoulders. With that, Zorvut stood and made his way toward the staircase, disappearing up the steps.

The barkeeper glanced over at Taegan as Zorvut walked away, a slightly curious lift of his eyebrow the only expression of emotion he had displayed so far.

"Awful friendly for a half-orc," he remarked. Taegan pursed his lips and nodded, glancing down into his cup of water. The less anyone knew about them, the better. "You must be payin' him well."

Taegan hesitated, then agreed with another nod. "Of course. He's a very skilled fighter and has never let me down."

The man whistled, wiping clean the wine goblet he had just emptied and rinsed. "Oh, I'm sure. Even the most desperate bandits wouldn't want to square up with a big fella like that. That's a good choice, even considerin'... Well, you know."

"Of course," Taegan agreed again, though he had no idea what the man was implying. It was a toss-up whether he was making some slight against orcs in general or perhaps the ongoing conflict between orcs and elves. Either way, he would be glad when the conversation was over.

As if answering his silent prayer, Nessie emerged from around the corner, carrying a clean towel with her.

"Mr. Alain," she said with a cheerful grin. "The bath's all ready for you, good and hot. Right this way."

"Thank you very much," he breathed with relief, hurrying after her.

"We're lucky enough to have a soap-maker in the next town over," she prattled in the mindless sort of tone that indicated she'd repeated the same thing in the same way a thousand times before. "So we've got a few different scent options, and it's not the hard scentless stuff you'd have to order in from the city in bulk. We've got rose, lavender, and spearmint. The spearmint's my favorite, if you ask me."

They followed the hallway around a corner to a wooden door which she pushed open, revealing a small tiled room with a decent sized copper bathtub, a shelf stacked with trays of bars of soap, and a table with a few folded towels. The tub was filled to the brim with water and steaming with heat.

"Now there's the bucket for rinsing, a clean robe for you, and a tray to put your dirty clothes," she continued, pointing around the room. "We don't have a full laundry service, begging your pardon, but plenty of guests just wash their clothes in the bathwater once they're done. Any towels or robes you use, you can leave here or in your rooms, we'll clean it up. Now if your manservant wanted a bath too, I can go haul out the oversize tub, so just let me know. Anything else I can get for you?"

"No, thank you very much," Taegan replied, and to her credit, the woman seemed to recognize his eagerness for her to be gone as she simply smiled and nodded.

"Just give us a shout if you need anything else," she said as she turned to go and closed the door behind her. It took only an instant for Taegan to peel off his clothes and immerse himself in the water, sending the overflow splashing down onto the tile.

The warmth of it alone was comforting beyond measure, and he closed his eyes in a brief moment of bliss. It was nowhere near as comfortable as his bath at home—he had to bend his legs to fit so his knees couldn't be fully submerged, and he missed the familiar scent of rosewater he would often bathe in. But compared to a week on the road with no warm water at all, it would certainly do for now.

He reached for the soap, going for the faintly pink-tinted bar in hopes the rose scent would be close enough, but even as he brought it up to his face, the floral scent was barely detectable at all. A frown of disappointment crossed his lips as he put it back, instead reaching for the pale green soap. Luckily, the mint was a stronger scent, and he set to work scrubbing away the grime and sweat and dust of the past week.

By the time he had cleaned up, though, the novelty of it was wearing off and was replaced with the same bone-deep homesickness he had only just been able to put a name to. He missed his own bath. He missed his own room, his private quarters, their leisurely walks around the garden. The thought of it was so painful his eyes welled up with tears, which only made him feel more ashamed.

He liked to think he was not spoiled, but the more logical part of him knew that he *must* be—how could he not be spoiled, as a prince, the heir to the throne, an only child at that? He felt so foolish to be upset that it wasn't *his* bath, but here he was, a spoiled brat crying over a lack of rosewater in a too-small bathtub. All he wanted was to go home. He tried to pull his thoughts away from the bond, shielding it from his outburst; somehow it felt even more embarrassing to think of Zorvut sensing his moment of weakness.

Taegan let himself hold on to the homesickness for a little longer, until he eventually dunked his head under the water both to wash his hair and also to destroy any evidence of tears on his face. Then he got out and dried off, and after a moment of consideration, plunged his dirty clothes into the now-tepid water. It was only a quick fix, but the water was satisfyingly murky when he wrung them out. Wrapped in a plain white robe, he gathered his things and made his way out of the bathroom, up the stairs and to room eleven.

When he entered the room, Zorvut was sitting on the floor, but sprang up quickly as the door opened. It was a plain accommodation with just a small writing-desk under a single window in one corner, a chest of drawers and a clothing rack in the other. Centered on the far wall, there were two narrow beds in wobbly looking wooden frames, which Taegan realized with a slight smile that Zorvut must have pushed together.

"That was fast," Zorvut said, returning his smile, then hesitating. "Are you all right? You seemed... well, upset."

Taegan winced. He must not have been quick enough to hide his thoughts. "I'm all right," he stammered. "Just more tired than I thought, I suppose. And... I don't know. I just miss home."

Zorvut's expression softened, and he nodded. "Me too," he murmured, then gestured toward the beds. "I laid out clean clothes for you. I hope you don't mind."

Taegan's heart swelled and ached. It was a small gesture, but a comforting one. "Of course I don't mind," he said, shaking his head. "Thank you." He hung his wet clothes on the rack to dry, along with the robe, and put on the clean trousers and loose shirt Zorvut had set out for him.

"A bath sounds good to me too," Zorvut said, watching him dress.

"The innkeeper said she had a larger-sized tub for you," Taegan said as he buttoned his shirt, then hesitated. "Don't be too long. I was hoping we could... um..."

Zorvut raised an eyebrow at that. "The walls seem awfully thin for that, Taegan."

"No, no!" he protested, flushing with embarrassment. "Not *that*, I just wanted to... I don't know. Well, nevermind."

Zorvut tilted his head, seeming to consider his words. "Well, I'll still be quick," he said simply, and Taegan nodded. His cheeks still felt warm as Zorvut stepped out of the room.

When he was alone, he climbed into one bed and wrapped himself in a blanket, staring out the small window. There wasn't much of a view, just the trees outside of the inn. He watched them sway in the breeze, and imagined the towering trees surrounding the castle, the wooded path of the archery range, and the gentle swaying of the curtain of willow branches in front of the tree temple. When he let his eyes lose focus, he could almost trick them into seeing the familiar shapes.

He had dozed off by the time the door opened again, causing him to sit up and blink groggily. Zorvut had returned in clean clothes, his short hair still damp and sticking up in some spots, and he carried a tray of food with him as he entered. He grinned at the sight of Taegan, who sleepily smiled back.

"My love," he said softly as he closed the door behind him. "I brought you dinner. I know it's a bit early, but I figured we could turn in early too."

"That sounds great," Taegan replied, and they crowded around the small writing table to eat. Zorvut set out a selection of breads and butter, roasted vegetables, and warm meat from the tray. It was all rather plain and unremarkable, but it was more pleasant than the smoked meats and hardtack that had made up the bulk of their meals on the road.

"Are you feeling better?" Zorvut asked when they were done. Taegan nodded.

"I have one more favor to ask," he said after a moment's hesitation. "I want... Will you just hold me for a bit?"

Zorvut smiled, visibly stifling a chuckle.

"Was that all? You don't need to ask," he replied, his voice a low rumble, and in one effortless movement had lifted Taegan up and carried him to the bed. He laid down gingerly, shifting around the spot where the two mattresses were pushed together, and after some adjusting they settled with each laying on their sides, Zorvut's arms wrapped around Taegan, and Taegan's face pressed into Zorvut's chest.

"Your feet are hanging off the end," Taegan whispered, and he felt Zorvut grin.

"I'm used to it," he replied with a shrug. His hands rubbed soothing circles along Taegan's back, and he closed his eyes, relaxing into the embrace. After a long moment, Zorvut's voice came again, rumbling through his chest. "I'm sorry this has been so hard for you. I know it must be difficult to be away from home, from your father. But I love you very much, and I want you to know I'm thankful you came with me."

Taegan nodded, unable to find the words to respond.

"I don't know if I would have been able to make it here on my own," Zorvut continued. "But when you're with me, I feel strong. And brave. Like I can do anything."

"You are strong," Taegan protested, pressing himself closer to Zorvut's heart. "And brave. Even without me. But I... I'm glad I came too. I think I would be much worse off right now if we were apart. So I'll be okay."

He felt Zorvut kiss the top of his head in response, and he closed his eyes. The safety of his arms and the even, comforting rise and fall of his chest quickly lulled him to sleep.

Chapter Four

Taegan woke with a start while it was still dark. Zorvut must have gotten up to close the window and blow out the candles, and was now sleeping soundly next to him, one arm draped loosely around his waist. He gingerly pushed his arm away and sat up, glancing through the windowpane. The faintest hint of sunrise was peeking over the horizon.

He crept out of bed and lit a candle before dressing for the day. His hair was a mess; by the time he had brushed it out and tied it back, more light was coming through the window.

As the sunrise began to just barely illuminate the room, he heard Zorvut stirring as he was packing his bag.

"Taegan?" his voice came quietly. In the near-darkness, with sleep still tinging his voice, he sounded so vulnerable and soft, almost like a child.

"I'm here," he answered quickly, and Zorvut sat up to look at him, a sleepy smile spreading across his face.

The sheer bliss that came through the bond when their eyes met caused Taegan to stop and smile back at him. He had not expected such warmth first thing in the morning, but Zorvut's still-waking heart must have been glad to see him. "Good morning, my love."

"Good morning," he answered, stretching. The beds creaked under his weight, and that seemed to snap him into a more alert state as he carefully eased himself over to the edge of the bed and stood. "You're up early."

"Well, we went to sleep rather early as well," he replied, nodding. "I've just started packing our things back up. I would have brought you breakfast, but it seems I wasn't quiet enough."

"That's all right," he answered. "I'll start getting ready to go, and we can eat together."

Taegan nodded and resumed packing. Zorvut dressed quietly, just in the light of the rising sun coming through the window and the faint flicker of the candle Taegan had lit. He meant to continue packing, but couldn't help but watch the half-orc's muscled form as he pulled off his sleeping shirt and dug through his pack for a clean one. He seemed to notice Taegan's gaze and looked back at him with an amused smirk. Taegan glanced away quickly with a flash of embarrassment, trying to return his focus to the task at hand. But soon they were both dressed and packed, and by the time the sun had fully risen and the sky had become a pale shade of blue, Zorvut was pulling back the bed he had pushed up next to the other and they left the room.

Down in the inn's dining hall, it was empty and quiet, save for the woman who had checked them in last night, greeting them with another smile.

"Early risers, I see," Nessie chirped as they descended the stairs. "Me, too. Some breakfast before you're back on the road?"

"Please," Taegan answered, and Zorvut nodded in agreement. They were served a simple breakfast of bread and butter, cured meats, and a dish of scrambled eggs mixed with a variety of vegetables that, though rather plain, was certainly serviceable. She offered them drinks as well; Zorvut took another ale, but remembering the vinegary wine from the night before, Taegan only asked for water.

"We do have tea if that might be more to your liking," she said with a wink, and he chuckled.

"Tea, then," he agreed, and she brought it to him.

As they ate there came the sound of another person descending the stairs; the stable boy who had helped with their horses stumbled down, yawning and scratching his belly underneath a rough woolen shirt. He gave a slight start as he noticed them and hurried behind the bar with sudden purpose.

"Go on, go on," the woman chided as he snatched a roll of bread from her grasp. "Be a dear and get our guests' horses ready once you've had your breakfast."

"Yes'm," he said quickly even as he shoved the roll into his mouth and darted out the door with a lanky awkwardness only gangly teenagers could manage.

"So where are you two headed?" she asked idly as they watched him hurry toward the exit. "Not many elves and orcs getting along with things being what they are. No offense meant, of course, just that it must be important if you're working together."

"Well," Zorvut said quickly, sensing the spike of nervous energy the question elicited in Taegan. "I'm a half-orc."

"Oh, my apologies, then," she said, looking him up and down. "My, you're one of the biggest half-orcs I've ever seen, then. Gods! What are you, seven feet?"

"That's exactly how tall I am," he replied with a grin; there was some bitterness to it that only Taegan could feel. "If you'll believe it, though, I'm usually head and shoulders shorter than most full orcs I've known."

"Goodness!" she exclaimed, and the topic seemed to distract her enough from her original question that she did not pursue it. "We don't get any full orcs around here, at least not on the road. That must be a fearsome sight, then, if they're that much taller than you, sir."

"Oh, yes," Zorvut agreed, nodding. He regaled her with a story of an orc battle that Taegan was certain he was embellishing for dramatic effect, not that he could blame him for the effort. As he talked, Taegan sipped his tea quietly—while he, of course, considered Zorvut to be quite charming, he had not seen him working so hard to be this overtly charismatic before. But the woman seemed rightly impressed, her eyes wide and focused on him, nodding along to the cadence of his tale.

"Well, by the gods, I hope you two stay safe out there, then," she exclaimed as Zorvut seemed to wrap up the story. "I've never seen an orc raiding party this far south before, but there's a first time for everything, isn't there? And you, sir." She met Taegan's gaze, and he raised a surprised eyebrow at her. "I expect you take good care of this fellow. I know what the stereotypes are, so it's good you're able to see past it. He seems like a very capable and strong worker."

Taegan gave a wry smile. If only she knew! "Yes, he is. I believe I was just telling your husband yesterday that my friend here is one of the most capable and reliable men I've ever known." He did not need to look over at him to know Zorvut's mouth had spread into a shy grin at that.

Their breakfast done, she took their dishes and wished them safe travels, and they made their way out to the stable. Taegan could already see Ember saddled up and tethered to one of several poles outside the stable, but the boy seemed to struggle with Graksh't. The massive horse was stamping the ground nervously as the boy, visibly just as anxious, struggled to get the saddle adjusted correctly over his impressive frame.

"Let me," Zorvut said, and the boy jumped, noticing them. He took the saddle from the human's smaller hands and set to work, easily getting the horse outfitted.

"My apologies, sir," he said nervously, eyeing Zorvut up and down with no small measure of visible fear in his gaze. Taegan pursed his lips, watching silently. While the woman had been pleasant enough, he supposed not all humans would be as outwardly comfortable in Zorvut's presence. Whether that was because of the boy's youth or some silent prejudice, he could not say.

"Ready?" Zorvut asked, glancing over at Taegan and shaking him from his thoughts. He nodded and mounted Ember as Zorvut got onto his own horse.

"Safe travels, sirs," the boy said as they trotted out to the road, and Taegan gave him a curt nod of acknowledgement but did not respond. When they were a little way down the road, Zorvut glanced back at him with a curious expression.

"You didn't like that boy," he remarked simply, and Taegan sniffed.

"He didn't like you," he said. To his surprise, Zorvut laughed aloud—just once, a sharp and bitter laugh, but a laugh all the same.

"He was a child," he said with a shrug. "It is not surprising to me that a child would be afraid of the unknown. You heard it from his mother, they've never seen full orcs. I doubt he's met many half-orcs either."

Taegan scowled, but he couldn't argue with that. "You are much more forgiving than I would be," he replied, and Zorvut's amused grin softened somewhat.

"Well, if I wasn't, I would probably just be sad instead. So I'd rather forgive and forget," he said with a shrug, and turned back to look toward the road ahead of them. Taegan glanced away but gave a relenting nod of agreement, even though Zorvut could not see him.

Although they were out of the mountains, it was still a rocky, unpleasant trail through the last of the foothills. They would not see any more signs of civilization until reaching a farming village on the edge of the foothills at the end of the day. From what Taegan remembered of the map, they were around five days out from the port of Naimere, where Tomlin Whitmore was rumored to have retired. They had already survived a week; he could manage another five days.

The rest of their journey was largely uneventful, but they saw signs of life more and more often along the road the further into Autreth they traveled. Though the first roadside inn had been quiet, the next farming village was a little more lively, and they began to pass people occasionally on the way to the next town, largely merchants coming to trade their wares for food and sundry items. They were able to spend the night at inns for the following three days, which was a welcome respite as well.

Though they still occasionally received stares, it seemed mostly unremarkable for an elf and a half-orc to be traveling together. For that cultural norm, Taegan was thankful. Most of the major nations had claimed and reclaimed Autreth at various points in history, due to its central location and expansive land mass, and so it boasted a vast range of cultures and races within it. For the most part, they seemed to live in harmony, and here at least it was a matter of rote normality for the races to intermingle. It was uncommon to see a half-orc, but not any more uncommon than any other half race, and they were mostly left alone as they traveled. The foothills gave way to slight valleys and grasslands, and they followed the main road for a few days before breaking off to a southern trail that would eventually lead them to Naimere.

When they left the main road, they passed fewer and fewer people on the trail once again. Where there had once been at least one or two other travelers passing by them every hour or so, it slowly dwindled down to just a few a day, then to almost none. The foothills gave way to marshy grasslands, and on the fourth day they were hard-pressed to find a place to camp that wasn't muddy and unpleasant, but eventually set their tent on a patch of grassy, mostly dry land a little way off the trail. Taegan's bedroll was still damp when he woke up the next day, though, much to his chagrin.

Now that they were out of the mountains and the landscape was considerably more flat, there was little of interest as they walked other than the new range of wildlife in the marshes and lagoons they passed, and Taegan spent most of the time keeping an eye out for small game, shooting down a few waterfowl and two rabbits. Zorvut did not seem interested in joining him; he seemed to be pulling his thoughts away from the bond for most of the day, but occasionally Taegan would feel faint tremors of anxiety coming from him. But even if he could not feel it, the expression he wore when he thought Taegan wasn't looking at him did just as well to reveal his thoughts.

It was understandable—he would be nervous, too, if he were only a day away from potentially meeting his biological father for the first time. He tried to project calmness and compassion through the bond, and Zorvut glanced back at him with a wry smile but did not respond.

Finding a place to camp was a struggle that evening as well, with their best option being a small patch of less-muddy land surrounded by soggy grass.

"It's the last night," Taegan said with a sigh as they started to unload their gear. "There'll be an inn tomorrow. We can wash everything then."

Zorvut gave a nod of agreement, but his gaze was distant as he started setting up the tent. Taegan tethered the horses to a tall bush—trees had become few and far between here—and watched him quietly, holding their bedrolls in his arms. His movements were mechanical, tired, slow; his thoughts were evidently far from the task at hand. With a sigh, Taegan carefully set the bedrolls onto Ember's saddle and came up behind him, placing a hand on the small of his back. Zorvut gave a slight start, and glanced down at him with a confused expression.

"Everything all right?" Zorvut asked, clearly surprised. Taegan moved his hand in a slow circle, rubbing his back gently.

"I should be asking you that," he said. "You've been on edge all day. Let me help you set this up."

Zorvut sighed, glancing away with a hint of embarrassment in his face. "Okay," he agreed, and

Taegan helped him stretch the tent over the poles the half-orc had already placed. "I *am* feeling nervous," he admitted as they worked. "It's just unsettling to think that by this time tomorrow... I don't know. I'll either know who my father is or we'll be heading back already."

Taegan nodded. "That's understandable. Truth be told, I'm rather... apprehensive about it, too. But at least we'll have some answers, either way."

"I hope so," he sighed, glancing away. "He might not even be here anymore, if he ever even was at all. It was only a rumor I had to go off of, after all."

Taegan hesitated. The small part of him that wanted to return home more than anything else perked up at the thought, but the rest of him was ashamed for even feeling anything remotely like joy at that prospect. "Well, then we'll just have to find the next rumor and follow that," he said. Zorvut glanced at him with a wry expression, and Taegan knew immediately that *he* sensed it was all bravado, but he seemed to appreciate the gesture, anyway.

"You're right," he agreed with a nod. "Although maybe we could check in with the king first."

"Perhaps," Taegan said, recognizing the peace offering, though he was not sure if the prospect of going home only to immediately set back out on the road was much better. "I suppose it would depend on where the rumors lead us. But we don't know either way yet, so no reason to make any plans."

"True," Zorvut sighed, grimacing. "Though that's harder said than done. I keep telling myself there's no point in worrying about tomorrow for today, but..." He shrugged, turning his attention back to the nearly finished tent. Taegan could all but feel his mind flitting from one thought to the next, but whatever he was ruminating over seemed to be too difficult to put into words.

"I know," he said, more softly this time. "I wish I could make it easier. But if nothing else, we'll always have each other."

Zorvut smiled at that, a more tender feeling coming through the bond now. "We will," he agreed.

They finished setting up the tent, and Zorvut helped him unroll the sleeping bags and start a fire. They roasted the fowl and rabbits Taegan had felled. Zorvut didn't bring up his worries again.

In his own private thoughts, Taegan certainly understood Zorvut's trepidation, although perhaps for different reasons. This human who they believed to be Zorvut's father was all but a mystery to him, yet they would approach him from a vulnerable position, asking him for help they did not even know if he could give. What if the man denied his paternity? What if he had no magical ability of his own after all, or proved to be a poor teacher if he did? A smaller part of Taegan worried what the bard would think of *him*, the man married to his unknown son. Elves were known for fostering relationships between any combination of genders and much of the world would not blink an eye at two men together; at most, some might be taken aback at an elf and a half-orc as an unlikely couple but certainly would not protest—and yet there were always outliers, and there was no guarantee a human would understand or accept the marriage bonds of elves. All they really knew about this man was that he was a moderately successful bard, and had the fortitude to lie with an orc woman. Anything beyond that was conjecture. Maybe his adventurousness indicated an open-mindedness that would find nothing remarkable in their own relationship, but maybe not. Yet if Taegan ended up being the reason Zorvut could not connect with his father, he wasn't sure if he could live with the guilt that might bring.

But just as he had stated to Zorvut, there was no use in worrying himself over tomorrow's mysteries for now. He forced his wandering thoughts back to the present and leaned closer to his husband as they sat in front of the fire. Zorvut wrapped an arm around him, kissing his forehead softly. That was all he needed, tonight and any night. They would have each other, he told himself, and as long as they did, they could face anything that might come their way.

Chapter Five

Despite his bravado, Taegan did not sleep very well that night, though he could tell Zorvut fared even worse. He slept in fits and starts, waking often, and when the sun first began to peek over the horizon, he felt Zorvut shift next to him and get up with a weary sigh. Taegan tried to sleep a little longer, but the smell of Zorvut preparing a simple breakfast and some coffee soon dispelled any hope of any more rest, and he too sat up to face the day.

"Good morning," Zorvut said, noticing him stir. Already Taegan could feel the heated tremor of anxiety from his end of the bond. He came up beside Zorvut wordlessly, wrapping his arms around the half-orc's waist, and they held each other silently for a few moments. "The coffee's going to over-steep," Zorvut murmured, finally breaking the silence, and with a wry laugh Taegan released him.

They set about breaking down the camp after their light meal, and were leading the horses back onto the road less than an hour after sunrise. It was slow going in the marshy wetlands, but even if their pace was this slow the rest of the way, Taegan expected they would reach the port of Naimere well before sunset.

But soon the road curved a bit more inland, away from the lagoon, and from the map Taegan could tell the trail would curve to the southeast for a while before making a straight shot south to the port town. More and more trees peppered the landscape as they moved out of the wetlands, going from short shrubs, to thin trees, to tall and thick ones; some with leaves that splayed out in long, swaying fronds, others with thin, flexible branches, almost like a willow tree.

"Maybe we should have a plan for if things go poorly," Zorvut said suddenly, when the sun had reached its peak in the sky. "Maybe if he is there, but... doesn't want to help for some reason."

"All right," Taegan agreed hesitantly, frowning. "Well, what do you think the worst-case scenario would be?"

Zorvut seemed to ponder that for a moment. "Either he has some prejudice against me," he said slowly after some thought. "Or is afraid of getting involved once he realizes who we are, who you are. He either may try to hurt us directly, or may report our presence to... I don't know, someone who will be able to get word back to the warlord somehow."

"That would be bad. Well, maybe we can try to figure out his position about the war before revealing exactly who we are," he offered, though he was unsure how well that might work out. "If he tries to hurt us—well, I think that would be more unfortunate for him. I'm not worried about us being able to defend ourselves. If he is afraid of somehow being targeted by our enemies, we can promise him protection, or if he casts us out, it would probably be best to simply leave without protest."

"But I think he would suspect who we are the moment he might know we're married," Zorvut sighed. "Elves and orcs aren't exactly known for getting along. Even here in Autreth, I don't think elves would be particularly interested in a half-orc."

"Well... You're probably right about that," Taegan admitted with a grimace. That was one stereotype about elves that was unfortunately well-informed by reality. Kelvhan's words echoed in his mind—*elves should be with elves*—but he certainly had not been the first or only elf he had heard voice such sentiments. "Maybe we can pretend not to be married. Maybe we're part of an adventuring group. Or we're just... friends, and I'm helping you out."

"But if he agrees that he's my father, then he would know my mother is the warlord's wife. So then why would I not be with the clan?" he pressed. "If I had been cast out before, would I not have tried to seek him out sooner? I don't know how well I could keep up a string of lies like that."

"Then we just don't offer the information unless he asks," Taegan said. Zorvut still seemed unsettled, but did not reply, instead looking distantly toward the road ahead. "If he asks why we're traveling together, we're friends and I agreed to help you find him. If he asks how we became friends, we met when the war was over, and when it resumed, we left for our own safety. That's *technically* the truth, after all."

"Technically," Zorvut sighed. "Maybe it would be best just to be forthcoming. If things go well at first, it would be hard to backtrack on our story... And if he has some prejudice against us, I don't know if I would want to spend any time learning from him even if he were to offer it."

That was understandable, though it elicited some mixed feelings in Taegan. It would be a shame to have come all this way, only to turn back of essentially their own volition. But if he were the one in Zorvut's place, he would certainly struggle to accept help from someone who did not accept his husband, too.

"I don't know if we can really have a solid plan that will account for everything," Taegan finally replied. "I think maybe it would be best if we just hold back a bit until we're able to get a better grasp of his intentions, his character. And I'm sure that if you open the conversation with you being his son, it will be a while before he gets around to asking about me, or us."

Zorvut chuckled, glancing back over at Taegan. "I think you're right," he said. "Thank you. That makes me feel a bit better."

"And if he does prove to be a problem," he continued, and made a slashing motion through the air with his hand. Zorvut laughed aloud at that, shaking his head with a grin as he turned back to face the road. Taegan stifled a smile, though he was sure Zorvut felt his amusement and affection through the bond.

They kept traveling and eventually the path curved more to the south again. On the horizon, the image of buildings began to rise up, slowly growing larger and taking on a more defined shape and color. Another faint spike of anxiety came through the bond once the city was within sight, though it was much less than the nerves he had felt from him previously.

There was no proper gate to the port, just an open archway surrounded by a low fence. A single guard stood posted at the archway, but only gave them a bored nod as they neared it on their horses. Clearly, they had no concerns about who was entering the city.

"Pardon me," Taegan said as they approached, locking eyes with the guard who perked up slightly at his attention. "Could you point us to the largest inn in town?"

"Well, there's only two," the guard replied, eyeing them a little more closely. "The larger would be The Snoring Seagull Inn, though. If you just follow the main road, it'll be on the left in the center of town. The proprietor's an old broad called Miss Jade."

"Much obliged," Taegan said, stifling a laugh at the inn's name. They made their way through the archway and into the town proper. The smell of salt in the air was stronger now, and appropriately, seagulls were calling overhead.

"Did you want to look at a tavern?" Zorvut asked, curiosity tinging his voice.

"I figured it would be the best place to start asking around," Taegan replied with a shrug. "And if nothing else, we'll know where we can stay tonight."

"Good idea," he remarked. They followed the main path through the small town, passing by some residential buildings. Most had their windows open with curtains fluttering in the cool breeze, and a handful of people walking the streets watched them curiously as they passed. As a port town, they certainly had no shortage of sailors and workers passing through, but just two newcomers, obviously non-human and presumably warriors, arriving on horseback—he could see how that would be a bit more of a spectacle.

The inn he had asked about was readily apparent as they reached the town square. In a small city such as this, the town square was exactly that: a central area of the city which the structures were built around, a hub for travel and activity with a few peddler's carts set up in the vacant spaces between the buildings and the fountain that served as Naimere's focal point. To their left, as they approached from the main road, there was one building slightly larger than the rest with open doors and more activity compared to its surroundings. A sign hung over the door, but it was so weathered and worn that Taegan could not make out either its words or the crest—only a few faint streaks of what might have once been blue and white paint remained. But it was unmistakably a tavern, and almost certainly the inn the guard had described. Zorvut glanced over at Taegan, who nodded in affirmation, then dismounted and led Graksh't to a tethering pole outside the inn. A human man was leaving the inn at the same time, and stumbled at the door at the sight of them, his mouth gaping open like a fish.

"Gods!" he finally gasped, then seemed to collect himself upon seeing Zorvut's eyes on him. "Beggin' your pardon, sir—I just, um, ain't ever seen a horse so big before."

"Yes, he gets that often," he replied with a chuckle. The man nodded dumbly before finally stumbling down the walkway he had originally started on, still turning his head to gawk at him and the horse for a moment before turning around, shaking his head.

"So much for laying low," Taegan sighed, though he smiled as he said it. Once the horses were tethered, they entered the inn. The door opened to a narrow hallway, just low enough that Zorvut had to lean down to walk through. Papers and pictures plastered the walls of the hallway; the papers looked to be in varying states of disrepair, some looking quite fresh while others had clearly been there for a very long time with tattered, crispy edges. They ranged from advertisements to scribbled artworks to personal messages—but Taegan only eyed them briefly as they walked, and the hallway opened up into a dining hall. The ceiling here was higher, and Zorvut could straighten up as they entered. It was a large room, bustling and noisy, with long mead hall-style tables and benches taking up most of the space with a handful of smaller tables pressed up along the walls, and a long bar on the opposite end. A few people looked curiously at them as they came in, but for the most part, their arrival seemed unremarkable.

Behind the bar was a single figure, an older human woman. Only one person was sitting directly at the bar, but a few tables were occupied with people eating a late lunch or socializing. They were mostly humans, but a few dwarves were peppered throughout the crowd. The woman behind the bar was passing a drink to the man sitting at the bar, but otherwise did not seem rushed or busy, simply surveying the room and greeting them with a slight smile and wave.

"Well, shall we have a drink?" Taegan asked, and Zorvut nodded. Now that they were inside, he could feel his husband's unease, though his expression was as carefully stoic as ever. He led the half-orc up to the bar and they sat down.

"What can I get you travelers?" the woman asked, leaning against the bar in front of them. From this distance Taegan could now see her more clearly—the deep lines next to her eyes and mouth betrayed her age, as did the long gray hair she was wearing in a low ponytail. But she still stood straight and had a youthful grin as she eyed them. "Let me guess. Wine for the elf, and something stronger for your guard."

Taegan grimaced, trying to force his face into his practiced charismatic grin. "You're not too far off. Yes, wine for me, I think. And for you?" He glanced at Zorvut next to him, sensing his slight trepidation that mirrored his own, though his expression was still neutral and calm.

"Just ale," he answered gruffly, and the woman nodded.

"Coming right up," she said, and turned her back to them as she grabbed a glass and uncorked a bottle. She worked quickly and was soon presenting them each with their drinks. Taegan took a nervous sip, but this wine proved to be much more palatable than the sour drink he'd had at the first inn that had scared him off human wines so far.

"Thank you," Taegan said, sliding a few coins across the bar, which she deftly dropped into her apron with a slight jingle. "You must be the famous Miss Jade."

She laughed at that. "Ha! I don't think I want to know who's calling me famous, but yes, you'd be correct."

"If you've a few moments to talk, I was hoping you could possibly point us in the right direction."

"Well, sure," Jade replied with a grin. "What are you looking for?"

"We're looking for a *who* rather than a *what*," he said. A spike of anxiety came through the bond, and he projected calmness toward Zorvut as much as he could manage. "We're searching for a human named Tomlin Whitmore. We're not entirely sure if this is where he is, but this is where the rumors have led us thus far."

The woman's grin dropped slightly at that; her expression was not hostile, but had become decidedly less cheerful. Whatever that meant, Taegan was unsure.

"Well, the rumors led you true, I'll give you that," she said, placing her hands on the bar and leaning toward them. "If it's an autograph you're looking for, well, Tom will probably give it to you, but he won't be happy about it. He came here to retire in peace, after all."

"I'm afraid there's a misunderstanding," Taegan said quickly, raising his hands in a placating gesture. "I'm aware of his previous exploits, but this is not the purpose of our visit. Rather, we've been sent to, ah, deliver a message."

"A message?" she asked, lifting a skeptical eyebrow. "And what might that be?"

"A message our benefactor believed Mr. Whitmore would be very interested in hearing," he replied, smiling wider. She sighed and shook her head, though the amused grin still lingered on her face.

"I can see you're not going to take no for an answer," she said, leaning back and folding her arms across her chest. "He doesn't live too far from here. If you head toward the harbor from the town square here, he lives in one of the tall houses with a blue tile roof. His is the one with yellow curtains. He's usually home this time of day, or out fishing if he's not there."

"Much obliged, Miss Jade," Taegan replied graciously, letting his face relax into a more natural smile as he handed her another coin. She raised an eyebrow at him again, but took it without comment.

"Yes, well," she sighed, rummaging idly behind the bar before retrieving a rag with which she began to wipe down the bar top. "I remember how it is to be young and adventurous. If you didn't hear it from me, you'd go bark up a different tree, and maybe this way I'll at least get some more of that coin you're so generous with by renting you a room."

Zorvut laughed at that, the first obvious reaction he'd had in their entire conversation, and Jade chuckled in response.

"Look at that! Made the tough guy laugh," she said, more to herself than to them. Taegan met Zorvut's gaze, and the half-orc managed a slight smile.

"Well, if we do end up needing a room for the night, we know where we'll find one," Taegan agreed. "In fact, if you have a stable where we can keep our horses, we might just take advantage of that now."

"Certainly!" she agreed, and leaned her head around the corner of the bar to yell up the stairs for a stable boy. "Vance! Come down here and help some customers with their horses!"

An irritated-looking boy of about sixteen emerged from the stairs a moment later, with dark wavy hair that flopped into his face. "Yes, ma'am," he said in a monotone voice.

"It's the biggest horse on the tether, plus the little red dun next to him. A stallion and a mare," Zorvut said. The boy hesitated at his appearance, then nodded. "You'll know them when you see them."

They stayed just long enough to finish their drinks. Zorvut was sipping his slowly, nervousness still simmering occasionally through the bond, but when Taegan downed the last of his wine, it seemed to kick him into action and he, too, finished off his drink in a few long gulps.

"Shall we?" he asked as he slammed the now-empty ale mug onto the bar, and Taegan raised his eyebrows in surprise.

"Let's go," he agreed simply, and Jade waved them away as they stood.

"Good luck!" she chirped, a wry grin on her face. Taegan wondered what Tomlin Whitmore must be like for her to have such obvious schadenfreude at the thought of them approaching him.

They walked out to the town square and along the southern path toward the coast. The glimmer of the ocean was visible on the horizon, and on the widest parts of the street Taegan could make out the shape of the harbor and some boats.

As they got closer to the harbor, most of the houses had a deep blue tile roof just as Jade had described, a pleasant contrast to the white stone the rest of the buildings were made of. It gave a decidedly nautical atmosphere to the cobblestone street. On the right side of the road, the buildings were taller and more narrow, and one had a set of yellow curtains fluttering through an open window in the cool breeze.

"That must be it," Taegan said, pointing to it, and Zorvut nodded. He paused, hesitating, and Taegan turned to look at him. His brows were furrowed and his gaze was locked on the narrow blue-roofed home.

"Let me do the talking," Zorvut said.

"Of course," Taegan agreed, nodding. Though he had been the one to act as their spokesperson for most of the trip, it only made sense for Zorvut to take the lead now. Taegan might have been the more chatty one between them, but ultimately it was Zorvut's quest for them to have ended up here at all.

Zorvut took in a long, steadying breath, and resumed walking toward the building, striding up a few stone steps to the door of the house with the yellow curtains. The door was wood, painted white to match the building, but streaks of pale brown were showing through where the paint was weather worn and chipping.

"Here we go," Zorvut said, barely above a whisper, and raised his fist to knock on the door—three solid knocks in rapid succession.

"Coming!" a voice called from inside. It was clearly a man's voice, deep and melodic even as he simply spoke. Taegan raised a comforting hand to give Zorvut's back a few gentle pats before pulling away as the door unlatched loudly from the other side.

Taegan was standing behind Zorvut on a lower step and couldn't get a good look at the human who stood in the doorway as it swung open, but could make out just a few features—a tall, skinny man with a short dark beard, a simple dark brown shirt and tan trousers.

"Can I help you?" the man asked after a beat of silence, obviously startled as he looked Zorvut up and down.

"Are you Tomlin Whitmore?" Zorvut asked, and his voice was even and calm despite the steady, staccato rhythm of stress coming from him through the bond like the tapping of a drum. The man's tense stance visibly relaxed at that, and Taegan heard him chuckle faintly.

"I am," he answered. "I take it you're here for an autograph? Let me find a pen—"

"No, we're not," Zorvut interrupted, and the man stopped halfway ducking back into the house. "I—we're here to deliver a message. May we come in?"

"A message?" he repeated, sounding surprised. "From who?"

Zorvut glanced back at Taegan nervously for a brief second before looking back at the human.

"May we come in?" he asked again, lowering his voice slightly. Something in his expression must have pushed the man into action, for he hesitated for just a moment longer before stepping back, pulling the door open wider.

"Sorry, I didn't see you back there," he said, leaning around Zorvut to catch Taegan's gaze. Now that he could clearly see the man's face, he was taken aback at how much like Zorvut he looked — the shape of his eyes and mouth, though of course scaled down on the human's smaller face, were identical to Zorvut's own. His hair had clearly once been dark but was now mostly gray, as was his beard, both of which were short and tidy. He was on the taller side for a human, and classically handsome with brown eyes that shone with an amber tint in the sunlight.

Taegan shook himself back to reality before his silence went on too long. "Not a problem," he answered with as gracious a smile as he could manage, and the man smiled back instinctively, though his confusion was still apparent in his eyes. Taegan followed Zorvut into the house, and the human closed the door behind him.

"Why don't you have a seat?" he said, brushing past them and leading them into a small kitchen on the left, where the window with the yellow curtains was located. There was a small dining table as well, but with only two chairs. "It might be a bit small for you, my tall friend, I apologize. Have a seat, please, and I'll bring in another chair. Something to drink?"

"No, thank you," Zorvut answered as he carefully sat down. As Tomlin said, the chair was decidedly too small for him and creaked under his weight. Taegan sat as well, and they waited in an awkward silence for a moment. It was a comfortable-looking kitchen, with white tile flooring and blue accents of dishes and wall art to mirror the white and blue motif of the surrounding buildings. A few fresh flowers were in a vase of water on the table next to them, and the stove was off, although the kitchen was a bit warm and had the aroma of a meal recently prepared.

Tomlin Whitmore emerged from the entryway with a stool which he placed opposite them on the table and perched on, a smile on his face, though his posture was nearly as tense as Zorvut's.

"Well, what's this important message, then?" he asked, looking between the two of them. Taegan glanced over at Zorvut, who was looking at him, and nodded encouragingly.

"Well," Zorvut replied slowly. "My name is Zorvut the Relentless, from the clan Bonebreaker. I came here to tell you... My mother is Naydi, wife of Hrul Bonebreaker. But I learned, not long ago, that the warlord is not my father. She says that... that you are my father."

Taegan's gaze had been on Zorvut, but once the confession was in the open, he glanced over to the human. His brows had raised incredulously, and for a drawn-out moment he was perfectly still until he finally leaned back in his seat, very slowly, and lifted a hand to cover his mouth.

"By the gods," he breathed, his eyes locked on Zorvut. "I didn't—I mean, yes, I remember Naydi, but... I had no idea. Gods!" He rubbed his beard nervously, and finally let out an incredulous laugh. "I'm sorry. I don't know what to say."

"Of course," Zorvut replied, sounding just as nervous. "I, um, I only found out a little while ago. It was a shock for me, too, certainly."

"A son," Tomlin said, shaking his head. "I have a son. Gods! How do you say your name again? Zor-vit?"

"Zorvut," he answered.

"Zorvut," the human repeated, and he laughed again. "Wow. Well, to be honest, this has never happened to me before, all the stereotypes about bards aside. Although I can't say I'd be surprised if there are a few more of you, none have ever come to find me like this. Well, it's good to meet you, Zorvut. May I?" He stood and extended his arms. A rush of incredulous surprise flooded the bond, but slowly Zorvut stood and took a step closer to the human. They embraced awkwardly for a brief moment, the human's arms not quite able to fully wrap around Zorvut while he patted Tomlin's back carefully.

Once they stepped away from each other, Tomlin looked up at Zorvut with his hands on his hips. "How long will you be in town, then? I'd love to get to know you, maybe go on a bit of a fishing trip..."

"Ah, well..." he started, then trailed off anxiously. "I came here for another reason, too. Around the same time I learned about you, I, ah, discovered some latent magical ability. Most orcs don't really have much in the way of magic, and I haven't been able to find a suitable teacher, so... we traveled here in hopes you might provide some guidance, or even just point me in the direction of someone who can."

"Magic!" the man exclaimed, surprise overtaking his face again, and there was a tinge of delight in his voice now that had not been there before. "Well, magic definitely runs in the family. My father had some ability with the arcane, as did his father. I've been blessed with no small talent as well. I can definitely help you out, though if you're, ah, traveling with elves, I'm surprised they haven't been able to help you more."

Taegan grimaced, speaking for the first time. "Unfortunately, sir, I have little in the way of magic myself. Hence our journey to come find you."

"I'm sorry, I don't think I caught your name," Tomlin said quickly, seeming to truly look Taegan over for the first time.

"I'm Taegan," he replied. "Pleased to meet you."

"And you as well, Taegan. And I must thank you for accompanying Zorvut all the way here. I'm sure it was a dangerous journey, things being what they are in the world."

He chuckled, nodding. The man didn't know the half of it. "I'm happy to help."

"But as far as magic, sure," Tomlin said, turning back to Zorvut. "I don't know how good of a teacher I'd be, but I'd be happy to help however I can. Do you have a place to stay?"

"We have a room for the night at The Snoring Seagull," Taegan interjected quickly.

"Ah, well, Miss Jade is a lovely woman," Tomlin chuckled. "I can prepare rooms for you if you'd like to stay with me for a bit after tomorrow."

"That would..." Zorvut trailed off and glanced over at Taegan again, a hesitant look crossing his face. "I think... Maybe you should tell him."

"Tell me?" Tomlin asked, glancing between the two of them. A faint grin lingered on his features, though it had fallen a bit, seemingly still unsure about them despite his warm demeanor.

Taegan nodded slowly, then looked back to the human. "There is more to the story, Mr. Whitmore. My name is Taegan Glynzeiros, and I am the prince of Aefraya, the son of King Ruven Glynzeiros. And Zorvut..." He glanced over at the half-orc, who gave a tiny, imperceptible nod. "Zorvut is my husband."

Tomlin looked between the two of them, his grin slowly dropping until his mouth hung open. "Oh, gods," he gasped. "You're the elven prince. Then you're the half-orc, and..." He stumbled back to his seat, leaning against the stool. His hand came up to cover his still-agape mouth, running his fingers nervously along his beard. "That's why the orcs declared war again. Gods, you're married? You can't be more than, what, seventeen?"

"Nineteen," Zorvut replied dryly. "But we consider orcs adults at fifteen."

Taegan blinked, pulling his surprise away from the bond. He knew Zorvut was a young adult, like him, but had he really not asked his actual age before? Nineteen felt strangely young even if he was an adult—but now was certainly not the time. That would be a conversation for another day, he supposed.

"And you," Tomlin stammered, looking at Taegan once again. He stood quickly, his face taking on a panicked expression. "You're a—I am *so* sorry, I've just never had a—a prince! A prince in my *house.*"

"Please," Taegan chuckled, raising a placating hand. "It's quite alright. And, you know, Zorvut is a prince as well, by extension."

The baffled human looked between the two of them for a long moment, then burst into a loud, nearly hysterical laugh before covering his mouth with both of his hands and sitting back down.

"I have a son," he whispered, seemingly more to himself than to either of them. "I have a half-orc son. And he's a prince, and he's married to the prince of the fucking entire elf kingdom. Gods help me."

"I understand it's a lot to take in," Zorvut offered cautiously, still sitting with his back stiff and straight in the too-small chair. He had hardly moved during the entire exchange; Taegan could feel trepidation coming from him more than anything else, though he was certainly feeling a wide range of emotions all at once. "Like Taegan said, we'll stay at the inn for tonight, and you can think everything over. Then we can come back tomorrow and decide what you'd like to do?"

"Of course, of course," Tomlin answered, nodding without meeting his gaze. "I mean, you can certainly stay here, and I'll do whatever I can to help, but you're right, this is a lot for one day." He ran a hand through his hair and shook his head rapidly, as if trying to clear his thoughts before looking at Zorvut again with a weak smile. Despite the tension that had just been on his face, his smile was instantly charismatic—the stereotypes about bards must have had some kernel of truth to them, Taegan thought. "Zorvut. Thank you for coming to find me. It couldn't have been easy."

Zorvut managed a slight smile, clearly disarmed by his words. "O-of course," he stammered. "Truth be told, I was very nervous going into all this. We didn't know if you would be... open to this, or if you would want to help me at all, or if you wouldn't want to get involved with, well... all this. I should be thanking you."

"Right, of course," Tomlin said, suddenly frowning again. "Is it—it's safe for you to be here, right? You're not being chased down or anything? I don't know much more except the orcs and elves are at war again. Are you in trouble?"

"No, I don't believe we've been followed," Taegan said, interjecting as Zorvut seemed hesitant. "It is an unfortunate possibility, but one we have taken many steps to avoid. If we believed we were bringing anything dangerous to town, Mr. Whitmore, we would not have led it to your doorstep."

"Please, you can both call me Tom," he said with a wave of his hand. "And that's good to hear. I mean, I would still want to help, certainly, but... Well, I wouldn't want to endanger anyone, either, of course."

"Of course," Zorvut echoed. "I agree. There were no signs we were being followed."

"In that case, please, I'd love to host you here for a little while," he said, then started laughing again, shaking his head in disbelief. "What a day! By the gods, I have a son. A son!"

The discussion began to fizzle out from there, both of them unsure of what exactly to say to the other. That was understandable; how often would anyone have a conversation with a father they've met for the first time? And learning he had an adult son must have been a shock for Tom as well, and his wide eyes seemed to continually dart back and forth between the two of them. Taegan watched their uncertain interactions as they tested the waters with each other with a faint smile on his face. Despite their awkwardness, there was a clear magnetism between them. Now that they were facing each other and speaking, the resemblance between them was only more apparent, which still amazed Taegan.

Eventually they sat in awkward silence for a long moment, at which point Taegan decided he needed to guide the conversation.

"I must thank you again for your hospitality toward us, Tom," he said, standing up. "You certainly did not owe us anything, but you've been exceedingly generous. I think I can speak for both of us when I say we truly appreciate it."

"Of course, of course," the human said, standing as well, his back stiffening. He was clearly even more unsure how to act around Taegan, despite his reassurances. "It's been a shock, certainly, but I'm glad to have you here. I'm glad to have met you, both of you."

"I think now is a good time to take our leave," Taegan continued, glancing back at Zorvut as he spoke. "To give you some time to process, and we can reconvene tomorrow. Does that sound agreeable to you?"

"Oh, yes. That'll give me time to tidy up my guest room," Tom continued, glancing up toward the ceiling—as tall and narrow as the house was, Taegan imagined most of the living quarters were probably on the higher level. "Please, come back tomorrow. I'll be here."

They agreed to return before noon the next day, and with one last uncertain but earnest embrace, Taegan and Zorvut took their leave, stepping back out onto the street. Taegan could feel the human's gaze lingering on them for a long moment before he heard the wooden door close as they headed back the way they came.

"That went well," Taegan said as they walked, and Zorvut nodded quickly. Taegan felt bond quivering with contained energy, buzzing with excitement, but Zorvut was the perfect picture of restraint. From his outward appearance, he seemed no more energized and excited than usual, yet just under the surface, he was roiling with clamped-down emotions. The half-orc briefly met his gaze, now barely stifling a grin. They would talk more in the privacy of their room at the inn.

"So how'd it go?" Miss Jade asked with a smirk as they returned to the tavern. Taegan returned her grin with a self-satisfied smile of his own.

"Very well, thank you," he replied, bowing his head graciously. She hummed in acknowledgment, but her gaze became decidedly suspicious, and she watched them with curious eyes as they headed up the stairs to the room they had rented. It was nicer than the roadside inns and village taverns they had stayed at on their journey, a little bit bigger, but still a far cry from their own quarters in the castle at home. The white and blue motif seemed to permeate the entire town, as the room had plain stone flooring and white-painted walls, but the wooden furniture was also painted white, and deep cerulean curtains hung on the window, the same oceanic blue as the sheets and pillows on the two beds. Taegan had not quite had the courage yet to ask for just one bed, but Zorvut did not seem to mind much either. Hopefully, it would be the last night they would sleep on two beds pushed together.

"I can't believe how well everything went," Zorvut said breathlessly the moment the door closed behind them, hardly able to contain the words any longer. "That was really... The best-case scenario in every way.

Gods, Taegan, I was so worried he'd kick us out of his house or—or chase us out of town, or worse."

"Yes, that went about as well as anyone could have hoped for," he agreed, a slow smile spreading across his face. Though Zorvut was clearly feeling a mix of emotions, the overwhelming relief and joy flooding through him was infectious.

"I almost can't believe it. I'm almost afraid to be too happy about it yet," Zorvut sighed, running a hand through his short-cropped hair. Taegan nodded slowly.

"That's understandable," he said, but Zorvut continued as if hardly hearing him.

"It doesn't feel real," he said, pacing around the room—it was small enough he could only get three, maybe four steps before needing to turn back around. "Like... I could wake up tomorrow and it could all have been a dream. That was real, right?"

"Yes, it was real," Taegan laughed, nodding. He sat down on the bed, watching Zorvut in fascination. He could not think of a time he'd seen the half-orc so moved—at least, not since their emotional reunion and re-bonding. "But I understand. I'm still a little hesitant as well, to be honest. There's no guarantee he might not change his mind come tomorrow morning. He did seem a bit nervous about us bringing danger into town, after all."

"No, no, I don't think he will," Zorvut answered quickly, waving his hand. Taegan stifled the tiny spike of irritation he felt at the gesture. It felt too much like being waved away, but he told himself Zorvut was just excited, eager—could he blame him for that at a time like this? "He seems like a man of his word. And if he can teach me more magic, I'm sure he can hold his own."

"Well, I hope you can learn much from him," Taegan replied, and when Zorvut met his gaze, his eyes softened into a more tender smile. Everything else seemed to melt into the background when Zorvut looked at him with the eager, hesitant smile that curled around his tusks, brightening up his golden-yellow eyes like a beam of sunlight. "This entire trip will have been worth it if you can learn something worthwhile."

"Thank you for coming with me," Zorvut said breathlessly. He stepped toward Taegan and fell to his knees, wrapping his arms around the smaller elf and pressing his face into Taegan's lap. "Thank you, thank you."

"You don't need to thank me, my love," Taegan chuckled, gently stroking Zorvut's hair and trailing his fingers along his cheek when he glanced back up at him. "But, I did want to ask you... Are you really only nineteen?"

There was a beat of silence between them, then Zorvut laughed aloud, the tension in his muscles all suddenly breaking at once as he leaned harder into Taegan affectionately.

"Yes," he said, shaking his head incredulously. "Yes, but I'm almost twenty, and orcs are considered adults at fifteen. I promise I wasn't a child bride."

"Well, that only makes me feel a little better," Taegan teased, chuckling. "I can't believe I never asked you something so... basic before."

"It never came up," he replied with a shrug, then raised an eyebrow. "How old are you?"

"Twenty-six," he answered with a grimace. "Though elves aren't really considered full adults until twenty-five, so in a way you've been an adult longer than me. Still, though... Nineteen!"

They had dinner still in the effervescence of the successful day, their joy echoing back to the other and building upon itself. The inn had a nice bath, and they were each able to wash away the lingering grime of their journey before turning in for the night.

Zorvut fell asleep quickly, clearly crashing after having spent so much of the past few days in nervous anticipation. But Taegan laid awake beside him for the long time, watching the flicker of shadows in the candlelight against the wall.

Now that he was in the quiet of his own thoughts, his own worries slowly crept back in. What if the man *did* change his mind? Or worse, what if they had been followed after all? Would Tom chase them out at the first sign of trouble? And what if he could not really help Zorvut, no matter how hard he tried? The warlocks of the elf capital had tried to guide him but were unsuccessful—who could say this human had any better way of teaching him than they did? He had not shown them any magic while they were there, had offered no proof of what he was capable of doing.

But if nothing else, Zorvut had been able to meet his father. The satisfaction of that, alone, would make all of this worth the trip, he told himself. The thought echoed in his mind until he could finally drift off to sleep.

Chapter Six

Though he had struggled at first, Taegan slept soundly through the night and woke to the sound of Zorvut packing their things. The half orc was already dressed, some of the same nervous energy from the previous day still lingering on him as he folded up their washed clothes and sorted their packed belongings.

"Good morning," he said briskly as he noticed Taegan stirring awake. "I went and spoke to Miss Jade about our horses. We can rent stalls in the stable for Ember and Graksh't, since it didn't seem like Tom had space for horses. I've already paid for the week for them."

"A productive morning," Taegan remarked with a yawn. "Was she surprised to hear we would be staying with Mr. Whitmore?"

Zorvut chuckled, though his gaze remained on the shirt he was folding. "Yes. I dare say it was one of the few times in her life a woman like that has been speechless.
"

"It's a shame I missed it," he laughed. "I apologize if I've overslept. "

"Not at all. I woke early and couldn't get back to sleep. I'm just glad I didn't wake you. No rush."

Taegan dressed and prepared for the day, and by the time he was ready to go down for breakfast, Zorvut had packed everything up and the room was bare once more. When they arrived down in the dining hall, the familiar figure of Miss Jade greeted them.

"You'll have to tell me your secret, elf boy," she said as she set down plates of food in front of them, what appeared to be steamed fish atop a bed of rice and a light vegetable broth. "How did you sweet talk old Tomlin into letting you stay with him?"

Taegan gave her his most honeyed smile, dripping with over-the-top, insufferable charisma. "Our benefactor is nothing if not persuasive, ma'am. Though Mr. Whitmore has extended his offer out of the kindness of his heart."

"Psh!" she snorted at that. "Just as likely he owes you. I always figured, a man that well traveled in that lifestyle for so long... of course he's got a past that would catch up to him eventually."

Taegan narrowed his eyes as he maintained the same smug smile. It was astounding how close to the truth she was circling, yet how far from it her assumptions were. But perhaps that could play out in their favor; let her imagine whatever sordid business they had gotten Tomlin Whitmore involved in, and maybe that would be a deterrent to snooping any further.

"All men have a past, that's certainly true," he agreed in as conspiratorial a tone as he could manage. "And a man of that renown, well, that's a safe assumption to make, Miss Jade."

"But you're not going to tell me why you're here, are you?" she asked with an equally conspiratorial smirk. "Yet, at least."

"Yet," he agreed, hoping the mysterious air wouldn't come back to bite him in the rear.

Once their meal was complete, they set out from the inn and strolled through the town square toward Tomlin's home. It was a picturesque morning, perfectly temperate with a comfortable breeze, and only a few streaky clouds breaking up the deep cerulean of the midmorning sky. They walked a bit closer this time, though there was still a safe distance between them. He missed being able to walk hand-in-hand with his husband, but the safest option while they were here would still be for as few people as possible to know who they were. If they could limit that to just Tomlin Whitmore, Taegan knew he would sleep a little easier at night.

So they walked a polite distance apart, though he kept Zorvut's nervous excitement cradled in his mind. It was not a long walk, so even at their leisurely pace, they were soon knocking on the white wooden door again with the yellow curtains fluttering out from the kitchen window.

"Welcome, welcome!" Tom exclaimed as he opened the front door with a flourish of his hand. A wide grin was plastered on his face; there was some clear showmanship in his sing-song voice and the sweeping bow he made as he stepped back, ushering them indoors. Taegan chuckled nervously, as did Zorvut.

"Thank you," he said as they walked inside, and Tom closed the door behind them.

"This way," the man said, squeezing ahead of them in the narrow walkway to an equally narrow set of stairs. "Watch your step. Especially you, Zorvut, sorry, I think it's going to be a bit of a struggle up and down the stairs..."

"Not a problem," Zorvut answered, though as Taegan glanced behind him he could see the half-orc following him slowly and cautiously with his head bowed low.

A small landing on the stairs had a wide, sunny window facing the other side of the street, and a few plants were set up on a table in front of it, which Zorvut also carefully avoided. The second set of stairs led to a long hallway with four doors, two on each side.

"Lucky the house has more rooms than I need," Tom remarked as he led them to the far door on the left. "My room is the first one on the right, and the one across from you's the bathroom. Next to you is just another spare room, so if you need some extra space, maybe you could store some things there."

He opened the door to reveal a spacious, largely empty spare bedroom. The bed, though certainly still on the small side for Zorvut, looked far more plush and comfortable than the thin, hard inn beds they had been sleeping in for the past week. It had a window that looked out over the street, and a tall armoire made of a light, warm-toned wood. A writing desk and chair were in the corner, likely just brought in since it did not match the armoire, and on the other side of the armoire was a mirror mounted on the wall. Next to the bed was a bedside table with a small vase and a few fresh flowers. Tom had clearly gone to some effort to make the room comfortable and welcoming for them.

"It's perfect," Zorvut said behind him, echoing his own thoughts. He could hear Tom chuckle nervously as he stepped inside.

"Well, it'll do," he replied. "I couldn't do much with the place with just one day's notice, but I do try to keep things tidy most of the time, anyway. Here, do you need any help with your things?"

They did not really need help, but Taegan could tell Zorvut did not want to tell him no, so he handed over a pack containing some of their camping gear, bedrolls and their tent. The room was feeling decidedly cramped with the three of them in it, though.

"You know, I think I have a storage space downstairs that might be better for this," Tom said after a moment of them shuffling around each other. "Why don't I go take this, and once you're both settled in, Zorvut, we can get started?"

"Getting right to it, then," Taegan remarked with a raised eyebrow.

"That's fine," Zorvut said quickly. "Yes, we shouldn't be long."

Taegan carefully unfolded and hung his clothes, but Zorvut was done with his own pack swiftly, clearly eager to get to training.

"Go on," Taegan said, waving him away with a slight grin as the half-orc hesitated next to him. "I don't need help. I'll find you both when I'm done."

A nervous smile spread across Zorvut's face, and he knelt down to kiss Taegan, taking him a bit by surprise.

"I love you," he said softly, his forehead pressed against Taegan's own. There was a rush of heat between them, the moment unexpectedly tender—after all, he was sitting on the floor with a travel cloak in his hands.

"I love you, too," he replied breathlessly, starting to lean closer to Zorvut, but the half-orc pulled away with the same expression, though perhaps looking a bit more smug now.

"Don't be too long," he said as he got back to his feet and moved toward the door. Taegan shook his head, flustered, but chuckled despite himself. He was glad Zorvut was in such a good mood; it was infectious even without their bond, and it was a relief to see him cheerful after so many days of anxious uncertainty. His own reservations were still a nervous, cold knot deep in his stomach, but he could keep them firmly pushed away for now. Zorvut was happy, he told himself, and for now that was all that mattered. Everything else could be figured out later.

Once his clothes had been hung up to his liking (though many still had an inordinate amount of wrinkles, not that there was much he could do about it without a hot iron), he peeked his head out of the doorway. Neither Zorvut nor Tom were upstairs, though he could very faintly hear their voices. It sounded like they were outdoors, perhaps in a backyard, though he was not sure how large of a space was possible in such narrow, close-together homes like this.

He was in no rush to get downstairs, and instead padded across the creaky wooden floor of the landing to inspect the bathroom. It seemed comfortably spacious, about the same size as their room, with a decent copper tub, and a sink and toilet with running water. The bathroom was a bit plain but the few decorations throughout seemed tasteful enough; a dark navy rug on the floor, and a painting of the ocean hanging on the wall within a glass-pane frame. A small vase with a single yellow flower was perched on the sink in between the man's toiletries, and below the window hung a plant with trailing vines. He figured Tom liked plants and greenery—there had not been a room in the house without them.

Curiosity overtook him, and he went around the corner to Tom's own room. This bedroom looked much more lived-in and cozy, with an unmade bed the same size as theirs, a dark wood armoire and a desk stacked high with books and loose parchment. He seemed to have abandoned the white-and-blue motif in his own room; the walls were still white but his bedding was a deep maroon, matching the curtains that were currently open over his own window and the deep mahogany wood of his chest of drawers and his desk. Taegan could also make out part of a bookshelf, which seemed quite full of books and trinkets of all kinds, probably from his extensive travels, and a similar trailing plant with vines hanging from the top shelf down to some middle shelves but none quite long enough to reach the floor.

Taegan only looked in from the doorway, unable to bring himself to fully enter the room even though the door was ajar. From what he could tell, Tomlin

Whitmore seemed to be a well-off man, not fabulously wealthy, but certainly comfortable and enjoying his retirement after a successful and profitable career. Nothing about him appeared particularly untoward or heinous, at least that he could tell. Though he still longed for his own home, this was not a terrible alternative for now.

Taegan stepped away from Tom's bedroom and opened the door of the other spare room, the one they were not inhabiting. It looked like it had been recently reorganized in a hurry, in a more noticeable state of disarray compared to the room he had provided them. It had a similar bed but no armoire; instead, a heavy chest was pushed up to the foot of the bed and a display case stood on the opposite wall. There were some instruments hung up on the walls, lutes and stringed instruments of various sizes. Inside the display case was some kind of flute, though Taegan did not quite recognize it, and next to the display case was a harp. He guessed this was normally Tom's music room, though he seemed to have repurposed parts of it for now; the chair in their room looked like it matched the wood of the bedframe and the chest in this room.

His curiosity sated for now, he quietly closed the door of the spare room and made his way down the stairs. From the landing of the stairway, he could hear their voices more clearly coming from outdoors, and could just peek into the backyard from the window there. It was as small as he had imagined, not much more than a patio with stone flooring and a few potted plants.

"Well, I haven't done anything too combat-heavy in some time now," he could make out Tom saying, his hands on his hips. "But I can definitely show you what I know. And maybe that'll bring back some of it. It really is like muscle memory, you know."

Taegan continued down the stairs, no longer able to hear their conversation as he moved away from the window. It took a moment of wandering downstairs to find the door to the backyard, but eventually, he joined them out on the patio as well.

"Everything unpacked?" Zorvut asked as he entered, giving him a bright smile.

"Yes, all good for now," he replied with a nod.

"Your, um—I mean, Prince Taegan," Tom stammered, glancing uncertainly between the two. "Did you want to join us? I'd be happy to teach both of you if you'd like..."

"Please, just Taegan," he replied, waving his hand. "And, no, thank you. I can't say I have much magical ability myself, so I'm afraid you would only waste your efforts on me. Zorvut is the one with the potential between us."

"Taegan. All right," Tom agreed, though his glance took on a bit of curiosity of his own. Elves were known for their magic; while not all elves had the same degree of magical prowess, he supposed he could not expect a human to understand the nuances of the elvish bloodline. "Well, you're welcome to sit out here with us, although it might get a little cramped. The door opens up all the way if you'd like to still sit inside."

He opened his mouth to say he had no need, but he met Zorvut's gaze and felt a faint tug at the bond, wordlessly hoping that he would stay. A smile played at his lips as he glanced away.

"I'll bring up a chair," he said, and went to pull one from the kitchen. A trickle of gratitude came from the bond as he did so.

When he returned, chair in tow, Tom and Zorvut had switched places, Tom closer to the open door now and Zorvut nearer to the gate. Taegan set up his chair just inside the doorway, leaning back to watch the both of them as the cool ocean breeze ruffled his hair.

"First, let's just see what it is you can do," Tom was saying, making a gesture with his arms for Zorvut to proceed.

"Right," he agreed, though his brows were now furrowed in visible concern. The half-orc seemed to ready himself, his stance widening slightly, then he extended a hand. After a brief moment, a flickering handful of flame appeared in it as if he were holding a candle.

"Not bad, not bad," Tom said, mimicking the gesture and quickly summoning his own handful of flame. "We can work on responsiveness, there was a bit of a delay... How far can you extend it?"

"Extend it?" Zorvut repeated; though his expression was blank, Taegan could feel his nerves mounting. "I'm not sure what you mean. I was able to throw it, once, the first time I used it, but... Since then, I haven't been able to do much more than just summon the flames."

"I see," Tom said, rubbing his chin. "Let's focus on that first, then. You said you threw it, but it helps me to think of it less as something I'm throwing and more an extension of my own hand. So try just extending it like you're reaching your hand out, instead of throwing it. Watch me." With a flick of his wrist, he summoned another small fireball in his hand and pointed at a slab of stone fencing in the alleyway between his patio and the building behind them. With a slow and deliberate movement, more like tossing a coin rather than throwing a weapon, the flame burst forth from his hand and streaked through the air to hit the stone wall, where it flickered into embers before dissipating entirely. "Now, you try."

Zorvut nodded, looking toward the stone Tom had aimed for. He shifted his stance awkwardly, trying to get into the same position Tom had used, before summoning the small flame in his hand and making the same gentle tossing movement. This time, it stayed lit once it left his hand, but did not quite make it to the wall, soaring only a few feet through the air before sputtering out in a puff of smoke.

But the bond still flooded with excitement and awe, and Zorvut looked first at Tom and then back at Taegan with a wide grin. "That worked," he said breathlessly. "Thinking of it more like that, it worked. Even practicing with the warlocks back at the castle, I couldn't get it to last—thank you, Tom."

"Very good," Taegan said, letting his pride filter through the bond. Zorvut had struggled with his magic for so long, it was heartening to see even a minor success now.

"I'm glad that helped," the human replied with a self-satisfied grin. "We'll work on that for today. Let's see if you can get it to reach all the way to that wall."

For most of the afternoon, they took turns throwing small fireballs at the wall. Luckily, whoever owned the fence either seemed to never notice or care, for no one came out of the building it was attached to. Taegan sat and watched for most of it, occasionally getting up to bring them some water or stretch his legs, but he did want to give Zorvut as much support and attention as he needed. It took a while, with Tom frequently moving to adjust Zorvut's stance, guiding him in the exact motions he had used, but eventually the half-orc's own smaller flame lasted long enough to sail through the air and strike the stone wall in a shower of sparks.

"Yes!" Tom exclaimed, clapping his hands. "Excellent, excellent. It will take some practice, but you're a quick learner. Very good."

"Thank you," Zorvut replied, panting. He was sweating now, between the heat of their fires and the effort of practicing for so long. He glanced at Taegan with a slight grin, which he returned.

"I think we're done for the day, then," Tom said, wiping his own brow. "I don't know about you, but I could go for a nice, cold drink about now. Do you have a preference?"

"Ale," Zorvut replied, following him back into the house. Taegan pulled his chair away from the door and closed it behind them as they headed for the kitchen.

"Dark? Light?"

"Any."

"Ha! Well, that's something you didn't inherit from me. I'll get a cold pint of my favorite dark ale for each of us. Did I show you the ice cellar? Here, it's this door in the kitchen. Goes right down beneath the house."

By the time Taegan had caught up to the kitchen, they had gone through the cellar door and he could hear their faintly muffled voices coming from below. That miffed him, but he tamped down the annoyance and waited politely at the kitchen table until they came back up a few minutes later, each with a heavy tankard of beer in their hands.

"Oh, my apologies!" Tom exclaimed upon seeing him. "What can I get for you?"

"I'm alright, though I wouldn't say no to a glass of wine," he replied with a wry grin. Tom nodded, squeezing past Zorvut to descend back to the cellar. When the door swung closed behind him, Zorvut set his beer on the table and came around to the side where Taegan was, embracing him.

"Thank you," he said softly, the words rumbling through his chest against Taegan's ear. He could feel the heat rising in his face, and even though Zorvut was damp with sweat, he raised his arms to wrap around his husband's torso, looking up at him with a questioning eyebrow. "I'm glad we made the journey here. I'm so glad you came with me."

"I'm glad you're happy," Taegan replied with a slight smile. The scent of his exertion sent a shiver of arousal through him, though he did not think their room was quite private enough for any such intimacy to be comfortable. Hopefully, they would not remain too terribly long. Zorvut's amusement from the bond only confirmed his thoughts, though the half-orc squeezed him a little tighter. *Later* trickled through his head, and he nodded wordlessly against his chest.

The sound of Tom clearing his throat loudly came from the other end of the kitchen, and they glanced over to see him coming up from the cellar door, looking down at his feet with a slight reddish hue to his cheeks. His embarrassment was apparent, and Taegan took a smooth step away from Zorvut, letting his arms fall to his sides. He was not quite sure what the man's flustered body language meant, but Tom held out a bottle of wine toward him, which he took.

"I hope you like white wine, since that's all I have at the moment, unfortunately," the human stammered, not quite meeting his eyes. "Here, let me bring you a glass."

He retrieved a wine glass from a cupboard, and after a moment they were all sitting around the small round kitchen table with a drink in hand, an awkward silence descending upon them. Taegan glanced at Zorvut next to him, who met his gaze and echoed his own uncertainty with a faint shrug. Tom was looking down at his tankard, and took a long drink from it before finally looking back up at Zorvut.

"Are you all right?" Zorvut asked, and Tom laughed with a grimace.

"Yes, yes," he said. "Sorry. I was, um, a bit confused to… That is—I don't really know how to say this. I guess I had figured since this was an, ah, arranged marriage…" He gestured between the two of them, his discomfort apparent on his face. "Forgive me. I don't mean to be rude. I suppose I had this idea in my head that Pr—ah, Taegan—was here more to keep an eye on things rather than, well, moral support. It surprised me to see such, um, affection between you two. Not that I..." He trailed off, biting his lip. "Well, I'm really digging myself into a hole here. I have nothing against you two, is what I'm trying to say. I guess I just had a preconception about you that was wrong."

"I see," Zorvut replied slowly, his brow furrowed. Taegan glanced between them before speaking.

"That's understandable," he answered quickly, leaning toward Tom over the table. "And, to be fair, I think it is a very safe judgment to make. After all, elves and orcs have been at war with each other for a very long time, and are at war again as we speak. I don't think Zorvut would mind me saying that if you had met us at the beginning of our relationship, your assumption would have been correct, Tom." He looked back at Zorvut, who was watching him with a neutral expression despite the mixed feelings of uncertainty and something like appreciation he could feel coming from the bond. "But Zorvut and I found we are much more compatible than I think anyone would have anticipated at the time the peace treaty was drafted. He has my heart, and I'm thankful for the circumstances that brought us together now."

Zorvut's lips slowly twitched into a faint smile, and he nodded in agreement. Taegan glanced back over at Tom, who was watching them with an expression of surprise that he quickly masked when their eyes met. "I understand the mating customs of elves can be seen as unusual by humans, but I hope you can look past that to see that we are indeed happy together."

Tom raised a placating hand hastily with a shake of his head. "No, of course. That's not it at all—I mean, who am I to judge? I've known a handful of elves in my day, and I have some understanding of your customs. Really, I'm glad that you're happy." He looked over at Zorvut and smiled—it seemed forced at first, but melded into a more genuine expression as he spoke. "The way I see it, being able to marry for love is always superior to a political marriage, but if you're able to have both, that seems like the best-case scenario. It's a relief to hear that, really. I was just surprised, is all."

"We are very happy," Zorvut said slowly, nodding as he glanced between the two. "Clearly, Taegan is the more eloquent one between us, but I agree with everything he said."

"Well, then," Tom said with a chuckle, and he raised his tankard. "To love?"

"To love," they agreed, and raised their glasses as well before drinking deeply.

"That went very well," Zorvut said with a sigh as they were in their room later that night. He had bathed and changed, sitting on the edge of the bed as Taegan sat at the writing desk, reading a book next to the flickering lantern he set up when the sun had set.

"What, your lesson? Or convincing him that you're not in a loveless marriage?" he replied dryly, though a grin played at his lips as he said it.

"Both," Zorvut replied, and he stood, stepping closer to Taegan. "You know, I wanted to thank you for, well, saving the day back there."

"Is that so?" he replied, raising his eyebrow. But his confident teasing faded quickly when Zorvut knelt down in front of him, grabbing the chair and pulling him toward his chest. "Wait, wait—I thought you didn't want to?" he hissed, glancing nervously at the closed door. He had no idea how much sound the simple wooden door might block.

"Now I do," he replied with a low growl. "I love to see you take charge like that. It's okay. You just have to be quiet, alright?" He unlaced Taegan's breeches as he spoke, and his hard cock springing free betrayed his protests.

"Wait—*ahh!*" he started, but trailed off with a gasp as Zorvut took his cock into his mouth, sucking him down to the base in one quick movement. Taegan pressed a hand to his lips, biting back a whimper of pleasure as the warm suction enveloped him. His other hand reached down to grasp one of Zorvut's tusks, pushing against him fruitlessly. He would not have been able to push the half-orc off him even if he had truly wanted to. He felt more than heard Zorvut chuckle around him at the weak effort, vibrating through his cock and forcing him to stifle another moan.

"Zorvut," he whispered, his eyes squeezing shut. "You—I—"

Quiet, he heard through the bond, and the word was so clear, so commanding, that he could not help but obey. He nodded silently, his eyes fluttering open to watch the half-orc suck his cock. The hand that had grabbed Zorvut's tusk moved to run his fingers through his hair; though it had grown a tiny bit in their time on the road, there wasn't enough to grab onto anymore. But Zorvut made a soft noise of appreciation, eliciting another muted whimper from Taegan.

It was so much harder to remain quiet than he had thought it would be—he was so used to being able to voice his pleasure without concern as the walls of the castle kept their noise contained, but the struggle of it and the danger of being overheard, of being caught still at the forefront of his thoughts, only turned him on more. Much as he would prefer Zorvut's hard cock filling him to the brim, this was a close second, his length surrounded by hot, wet pressure and Zorvut's tongue moving against the sensitive spot on the underside of his cock, sending wave upon wave of ecstasy through him. He thrust his hips weakly in time with the half-orc's head bobbing up and down, and the increased friction drove him to the brink. He clenched his hand harder in Zorvut's hair, holding his head in place as he came, his other hand still pressed hard to his mouth to stifle a moan. The half-orc sucked him through it, greedily squeezing out every last drop of come and drinking it down.

Taegan remained there, struggling to catch his breath with his eyes closed for a long moment. When he finally was able to open them, Zorvut had released him and was grinning up at him smugly.

"Now you," Taegan said, pushing his chair back to stand.

"Me?" Zorvut asked with a raised eyebrow.

"Don't be coy," Taegan said, glancing down at the hard bulge in Zorvut's own breeches. "You'll have to be quiet, too."

Zorvut laughed, shaking his head, but Taegan could feel his interest was piqued. The half-orc allowed himself to be led to the bed, laying down and lifting his hands to run his fingers through Taegan's hair as the smaller man crawled into the space between his spread legs. "I'll be quiet."

"Good," Taegan said, and pulled down the half-orc's trousers. There was no way he could get Zorvut's massive cock all the way into his mouth the way he had done with his own, but it certainly wouldn't stop him from trying.

With his mouth open wide, he was able to get the head of his cock past his lips, swirling his tongue around the thick member. Zorvut made a soft noise of appreciation, then seemed to catch himself, closing his eyes in concentration. If Taegan could smirk with his mouth so full he would have. Instead, he sucked as hard as he could, filling his mouth with as much of the cock as he could hold, both of his hands working up and down the rest of his shaft.

Zorvut's breathing was harsh despite the lack of tension in his expression, his eyes closed and his hands held firmly at his sides when he glanced up at him. If it were not for the pleasure arcing through the bond with each slight bob of his head, he might guess that Zorvut was meditating. There was an eroticism to his silence but the thought of being able to force a sound of pleasure from him despite his disciplined self-control made his own cock twitch in interest again. He gripped a little harder with his hands, feeling along the thick vein running up the underside of his cock, hollowing his cheeks with constant suction. One hand trailed down a little further to cup and squeeze his balls, eliciting a slight gasp and a hitch of his breath. Almost, but not quite.

Taegan could feel his cock hardening, feel himself wet with slick. He thought of Zorvut fucking him, the cock that was too big to fit in his mouth filling his hole perfectly, and tried to push the thought toward Zorvut as he sucked, letting his teeth brush lightly against the sensitive skin.

"Taegan," was all Zorvut said, his voice low and restrained as his head tipped back with his eyes still closed. He felt his balls tighten against his hands and his mouth was flooded with come, thick and hot. He swallowed hard, drinking down as much as he could, but still it spilled from between his taut lips, leaking down his chin. As the hot liquid filled his mouth and belly, he couldn't stifle the faint moan that escaped him. When he finally pulled away, he was still dripping with it, and Zorvut's eyes had opened to watch him.

"Gods," Zorvut groaned, barely above a whisper as one hand lifted to stick a finger in Taegan's mouth, eliciting another whimper from him as his mouth was pulled open, smearing his face with come. Their eyes met and the heat between their gaze felt palpable. Zorvut hauled him up into his lap and kissed him hard; Taegan moaned as the half-orc's tongue invaded his mouth, exploring every inch of where his cock had been and tasting the same saltiness he had given him.

When they finally pulled away, he could not ignore the wet spot of precome where his cock was straining against his loosely laced breeches—and neither could Zorvut, as he was pushing down his trousers again and started to stroke his over-stimulated member.

"Fuck," Taegan breathed, biting back a cry as Zorvut's other hand found his slick hole and fingered him.

"My spoiled prince," Zorvut whispered, stroking him hard and fast. "Always getting to come twice. You're going to come again for me, aren't you?" Taegan's hands clenched into fists against Zorvut's shirt, the fabric bunched up between his fingers in his struggle to stay quiet. Zorvut's words and rough hands sent him over the edge again, far too easily. He could only produce a few weak spurts of come that spilled onto Zorvut's shirt, but pleasure crashed through him in waves just the same, arcing from the stimulation to his cock to clench around Zorvut's fingers inside him.

It took a long moment for him to catch his breath, his cock still in the half-orc's grasp. He hissed when Zorvut finally pulled away, releasing his softening cock and pulling out of his hole with a slick sound.

"My love," Zorvut said softly as he leaned back with a self-satisfied smile. "I don't know if we should keep doing this. I don't think I can be that quiet every time."

Taegan stifled a laugh as he stumbled to his feet. "I would agree with you, but I think we both know that won't last long."

Chapter Seven

The next day was much of the same, though they had a leisurely breakfast with Tom in the morning before he and Zorvut went out into the small backyard again to continue their training. Taegan watched with idle half-interest from the kitchen, but soon busied himself with other tasks as much as he could. Now that they were safely settled in town, he retrieved a set of parchment and a pen from his belongings, writing out a letter to his father, as they had agreed.

It took a few scrapped drafts before he decided on a letter that seemed the appropriate balance between vague and recognizable to Ruven, so that he might understand what Taegan wrote to him, but any potential interceptors would not.

Dear Castien,

I write to you with tidings of good health. My partner and I have arrived safely in the port of Naymere where we will stay with his tutor while he begins his studies. No news from the road, as our journey was unremarkable in every way. We hope you are remaining just as safe, and this letter finds you well. I look forward to your response, but it is with greater anticipation that I look toward the day we will be reunited once more.

Sincerely,

T. G.

Satisfied with his work, Taegan tossed the scrapped letters into the stove where the embers from the morning's meal still glowed, and carefully folded the final draft of the missive into thirds and sealed it with a few drops of red wax. Now he would just have to find a courier.

He peeked through the back door where Zorvut and Tom were training—seemingly satisfied with fire for now, Tom was explaining to him the way to shift from summoning flame to calling down lightning.

"Forgive my interruption," he said quickly, the two men glancing over at him in surprise, and he held up the folded and sealed piece of parchment. "Tom, I wondered if you might know of a trustworthy courier service I might take advantage of. One that would be able to deliver a letter to Aefraya."

"All the way to Aefraya?" Tom repeated, running a hand along his graying beard. "Well, the courier I've used in the past has never given me any problems, but I'm not entirely sure they'll be able to travel all the way to the elven capital, times being what they are. If you go to the courier service in the town square, ask for Edwin. He should be able to help you out, or at least point you in the right direction."

"Much obliged," Taegan answered, and met Zorvut's gaze. "I'll be back soon."

"Be safe," Zorvut replied with a stern nod, and Taegan smirked.

"Always," he said as he walked away.

The day was still young, with the sun not quite having reached its peak in the sky, so Taegan walked leisurely as he stepped out the front door and out onto the street. A few workers were heading toward the dock, presumably returning to work after taking a break, but otherwise the street was mostly empty. He strolled on the stone path toward the town square, taking in the sights. A few gulls called overhead as they soared toward the ocean, and when he glanced up to look at them, he could see a human woman hanging laundry out to dry from the rooftop of one of the buildings. The nearer he got to the town square, the more lively the street became.

As he walked, he could feel Zorvut's range of emotions through the bond, a rhythmic cycle of focused concentration becoming either a tinge of frustration or a flash of satisfaction. It was a bit odd, being able to tell exactly how his training was going, even from this distance. The town square was less than a mile from Tom's home, though, so he was fairly certain they would remain connected.

In contrast to the quiet streets, the square was bustling with activity. The Snoring Seagull and the other small restaurants and food carts seemed calm so far, though the lunch rush would likely be upon them soon. Some stalls were set up in the empty parts of the square where merchants were selling their wares, calling out to the people walking along the stone paths—the stalls ranged from textiles and simple clothing to fresh seafood and other provisions.

Nothing looked immediately like a courier service, so he made a slow circuit around the square, looking at each door or sign on every building until he could finally track it down, a narrow red door without a window or outward sign but simply the word "Courier" painted on the red surface in clean black lettering. It was the only such one he had found, so this must have been the courier service Tom meant. He placed a hand on the doorknob, twisting it; it was unlocked, so he stepped inside.

The shop was a narrow and long room, with a few austere decorative items on shelves but rather empty save for the long counter that stretched along the right-hand wall, a dark wood that went pleasingly with the dark forest green paint on the walls. Behind the counter was a tall, gangly human man with a clean-shaven face, neat brown hair parted on one side, and large spectacles that gave him the appearance of some kind of very long insect.

"Welcome," the human said, looking up from some papers on the countertop in front of him as Taegan entered. "How can I help you?"

"I was told to ask for Edwin," Taegan replied, taking a few careful steps toward the man. The human glanced at his ears briefly, but if he was surprised at all to see an elf in his establishment, he gave no outward sign of it.

"That would be me," the man replied with a nod of his head. "At your service, sir."

"Excellent," Taegan said, and he pulled the letter from his cloak pocket. "I'm unsure what services you offer, but this letter needs to be delivered to the city of Castle Aefraya."

The man's eyebrows twitched but he bent down beneath the counter to bring up a ledger book without missing a beat.

"Hmm," he said, pursing his lips and pulling up another stack of papers. "Let me see what routes we have planned out for the month..." He shuffled through the papers and brought out a few maps, some which Taegan recognized and others, which seemed to be more local and narrow in scope, that he could not pinpoint. Each had a few routes highlighted in red with small notes scribbled next to them—the maps that he did recognize as Aefraya in did not seem to have any highlighted routes.

"Unfortunately, sir, times being what they are, we don't have any regular line going to Aefraya for the foreseeable future," Edwin said, folding his arms across his chest as he met Taegan's gaze again. "I can arrange an independent delivery for you, but it's much more expensive than going on the regular routes."

"Money is of no concern," he replied with a wave of his hand.

"In that case," the man said with a nod, and he leaned over the maps again, tracing his finger along the demarcated roads, his lips moving in silent mutterings to himself. "How soon do you need this delivered?"

"The sooner the better," Taegan said with a nod, and the man straightened up once more.

"For a courier on foot, I'd put it at about thirty-five gold coins. For a rush delivery on horseback, fifty."

"Fifty it is," Taegan said, though it was significantly more than he was hoping to spend. He pulled his coin purse from another pocket and emptied out fifty gold coins, sliding them across the counter which the man plucked up quickly, making a note in his ledger book as he deposited them in a small lockbox.

"Excellent," Edwin said once he had counted them all out. "Now, I'll take your letter, and I'll just need some information from you. Do you have an exact address of where it's going?"

"An inn in Castle Aefraya called the Magenta Marigold," he replied as he handed over the letter. On the side without the wax seal, Edwin noted down the name in the same red ink that Taegan had seen on the maps.

"Name of the recipient?"

"An elf called Castien."

"And if your recipient is unavailable? Is there an alternate recipient you would want it delivered to instead?"

"Whoever is running the inn at the time, then," Taegan replied with a shrug. It would be unusual for Castien not to be in the tavern, but it was possible the message might arrive while the man was off duty.

"And your own name, sir?"

Of course they would need his name. "Taegan... Glen—more," he stammered, quickly spitting out the first fake surname he could string together and hoping it was not too obviously similar to his own.

"Sorry, could you spell that for me?" Edwin said, his pen hovering over the letter as he hesitated.

Hopefully a different spelling would help too. "T-e-g-a-n," he said, trying to envision the least similar spelling to his own name. "Last name is g-l-e-n-m-o-o-r."

"Got it," the human said with a nod, jotting it down. "Well, payment has been tendered, so you're all set, Mr. Glenmoor. Pleasure doing business and I'm happy to help."

"Thank you," Taegan replied with a prim nod, watching with a faint tinge of forlornness as Edwin placed the letter onto a small stack of other papers and parcels, disappearing from sight. The gangly human waved goodbye as he left the establishment.

Back in the town square, he stood outside the closed door for a long moment before taking in a deep, slow breath and letting it out as a heavy sigh. He had nothing else planned for the day, so he decided to stop at the tavern for a quick lunch, then perhaps take a longer walk around town.

Miss Jade was behind the bar again as he walked in—he could not recall seeing anyone else at the counter in the handful of times they'd visited the establishment. She smiled in recognition as he approached the counter, raising a hand in greeting.

"Back so soon!" she said wryly.

"Just for lunch," he replied with a chuckle, glancing around the dining room before taking a seat. There were only two other people sitting at the bar, both of them visibly dock workers on a break, but a few small groups were sitting at the tables spread evenly through the hall. "What do you have available today?"

"Lunch special today's clam chowder and an ale for four silver coins. No substitutions on the drink, sorry," she said, winking. "I know how elves are about their wine, but we've got what we've got."

"I suppose I can try branching out," he said with a sigh, though his slight grin certainly betrayed him. She nodded as he set down the coins, and a moment later, he was presented with a large stone bowl filled with steaming, creamy soup and a mug of cold ale. The soup looked perfectly rustic, with big chunks of root vegetables swirled throughout and a generous sprinkle of pepper dotting the surface. He could not recall having a soup made with fish before, or any kind of seafood, but on the first taste found it quite pleasant and finished his bowl without complaint.

"I don't think I ever quite caught your name, Mr. Elf," she remarked idly as he took an experimental drink of the ale. At the first sip, it was much more light and refreshing than he would have guessed. "Your tall and handsome companion was the one who arranged everything with your horses, if I recall."

Taegan almost choked on his drink—though he did not disagree, he had never heard someone else refer to Zorvut as *handsome*. Humans really were known for their adaptability and affable natures, though, he supposed.

He was so caught off-guard he couldn't even come up with a lie. "I'm Taegan," he said once his coughing fit had subsided, though she was still laughing at him as he spoke.

"Is it that surprising to hear he's the handsome one between you?" she teased, shaking her head. "Well, I can't speak for every lady, but sometimes all it takes is being big and strong. Though he's certainly a looker, out of the half-orcs I've seen in my day."

"And I take it you've seen quite a few half-orcs?" he asked.

"Oh, yes," she agreed. "I got my start as a barmaid all the way out in Gennemont—that's the capital of Autreth if you weren't aware, and as the capital we got all sorts, oh, *all* sorts. A half-orc wouldn't cause anyone to bat an eye when there were half-dragon merchants from the northern tribes hawking in the town square and devilkin in all the gambling halls."

"I see," Taegan replied slowly, immediately regretting giving her his name. A well-traveled human was far more likely to be a well-informed human, and the last thing he needed was to be recognized by the woman who owned the biggest inn in town.

"Anyway," Miss Jade continued. "All that to say, I know a handsome half-orc when I see one, so you should keep a close eye on your friend, especially if he takes after old Tom."

If he had been surprised before, his heart had all but stopped now. "I—I beg your pardon?" he asked, hoping against all hope maybe he had misunderstood her.

"Well, I didn't connect the dots at first," she said, pointing at him with a wine glass she had been wiping dry. "But the more I thought about it, and when I saw him for the third or fourth time when you were checking out, it all just clicked. I can definitely see the resemblance, and for you to come looking for Tom only to end up staying with him—what else would it be? I know Tom pretty well, though, and fucking an orc woman wouldn't even top the list of the most scandalous things he's done in his wilder days. Probably in the top five, though." When she met Taegan's eyes again, she smirked, clearly taking his speechless expression for confirmation. "Very kind of you to help your friend track down his father."

"Yes, well," he stammered, though he had no idea what to say. "It was a hunch, but, ah, a gamble that paid off."

"Now, what I still can't figure out," she said, the grin sliding from her face as her voice lowered. "Is why the elven crown prince and his husband would risk coming here on a hunch instead of staying high and dry in their fancy tree castle."

The ale he had found so pleasant just a moment ago soured in his stomach. With a concerted effort, he smoothed his furrowed brows, keeping his face as carefully expressionless as he could manage.

"Perhaps the less you can figure out, the better," he replied coolly, leaning away from the counter. His heart was suddenly pounding so hard he was sure she could see his pulse thrumming through his skin.

But to his surprise, she chuckled again, turning away to resume her cleaning. "Well, you're probably not wrong. I haven't gotten this far in life by sticking my nose where it doesn't belong, after all." She glanced back at him, seeming to read the anxiety in his eyes perfectly despite his neutral expression. "Don't worry, I won't be sharing your little secret, though you don't seem too good at keeping it to yourself."

"Your discretion would be appreciated," he muttered, then took a long drink from his ale. "Was it that obvious?"

"Well, an elf and a half-orc traveling alone together is a bit unusual even in Autreth," Miss Jade said, shaking her head with an incredulous grin. "Just that by itself wouldn't have tipped anyone off, though, and your plain clothes would throw most people off the scent, too. But maybe don't tell people you have the exact same name as the elf prince married to an orc if you don't want people to know you just so happen to be that same elf."

"Taegan is a perfectly common name," he said with a shrug. "In fact, it's quite frequent for the names of newborn royals to see a spike in popularity amongst elves in the year or two after their naming. Many elves around my age would be named Taegan or some variation of it."

"That would probably work with most folks," she responded with a wry grin. "But, well, I suppose I'm not most folks. No need to worry, though, like I said; I don't stick my nose where it doesn't belong, and I don't go blabbing about someone's business that isn't my own."

A large group of sailors entered the tavern then, thundering through the doors as one was singing a bawdy drinking song and the others were laughing uproariously, pulling chairs up to all sit at the same table around the singer with his lute.

"Begging your pardon," she said with an overly sweet smile, and she left the bar to take their order. Taegan watched her for a long while as she greeted the group, smiling amicably at them and even laughing and smacking one man's shoulder when he gave her a flirtatious grin, though he could not make out the words. But eventually he shook himself out of his stupor, downing the rest of his ale and leaving an extra gold coin on the counter—though he partly trusted her word, buying her silence couldn't hurt either. He left the tavern before she could return to the bar, hurrying past the group without looking toward her.

The crisp ocean air would do well to clear his thoughts. He made his way through the town square, heading closer to the harbor but down a different street, one that let out closer to the strand rather than the docks. It was a touch warmer, the sun a bit higher in the sky, but still pleasant and breezy. This street was a touch more narrow, the residential buildings he passed a bit more cramped. Two children, human girls of no more than ten, were kicking a ball between them in the street and watched him curiously as he passed, but otherwise, this street seemed just as calm and clear as the street Tomlin Whitmore lived on.

The town square was just over a mile away from the coast, so he reached the beach before long. It was close enough to the docks that there were not any idle beach-goers in the near vicinity, since the noise of dockworkers shouting, the loud wooden creaking of ships, and the hammering of repairs were all still quite loud. He found a cluster of dark, craggy rocks that would have made a pleasant vantage point if it weren't for all the noise, and sat down to look out at the sea.

He had seen the ocean a few times in his life, but could certainly see the appeal of wanting to live somewhere it could be viewed at any time. Even with all the background noise, there was a soothing quality to the rhythmic, unending rise and crash of the waves, the calling of gulls occasionally breaking through from the clouds above.

When his head felt clear enough that he could actually think, he focused his thoughts on Miss Jade and their conversation. She seemed like a smart and insightful woman, but he could not trust that others he might come across in town were not just as intelligent. He had let his guard down and paid for it immediately; though part of him did not truly think she would break her word to him, it was still now a risk he had to consider.

He wondered briefly if he should try avoiding her altogether, but it seemed the safest place to keep their horses, so they would have to return to the inn at least once again, if not more. And it might seem more suspicious if he suddenly appeared to be going out of his way to avoid her; perhaps it would be better to play it off as of little concern to him, like he had nothing to hide so she had nothing to think too hard about. Though that certainly had the risk of backfiring, and she might try to wheedle more information out of him- —or someone else in the tavern might also make the connection and act less discreetly.

But he had to tell Zorvut, though he felt a slight trickle of shame at the thought. Maybe he would have a stronger idea of how to handle what had suddenly become a loose cannon in their hands. He had kept his emotions mostly pulled away from the bond, and luckily it felt as though Zorvut was still preoccupied with his training, so maybe any stray thoughts that had gone through had not been noticed. He supposed there was only one way to find out.

"You gave her your *name*," Zorvut said to him flatly when he returned from his walk later that afternoon, sitting across from him at the kitchen table. After their training, the three of them had gathered around the table once more for a round of drinks. Taegan winced at the flash of frustration that came through the bond at the words, and even Tomlin's raised eyebrows were a fresh stab of guilt.

"It's not that uncommon of a name," he protested, though the excuse was weak to his own ears. "But... yes, although she suspected it even before."

Zorvut took in a long, slow breath, looking down at his drink pensively. Whatever he was feeling, he was shielding it from the bond, but Taegan felt he could safely guess the half-orc was more frustrated than anything. "Well, that's not the worst news, but it's not great, either," he said slowly. "Maybe it would be best if you stayed away from this woman."

"You don't think that might be more suspicious?" Taegan asked, frowning.

"Suspicious? What would she suspect you of?" Zorvut countered. "She already knows who we are. The less she knows about you going forward, the better."

"I suppose you're right," he said slowly. He would miss the opportunity for socialization, but it couldn't be helped. "We'll have to go back to either get the horses or pay for another week, though."

"That's fine," Zorvut sighed, eyeing Taegan with a softer expression. He seemed to recognize Taegan's mixed emotions. "You don't think she means any harm?"

"I don't know. But I don't think so," he replied with a shrug. "She seemed more... curious, in a way. Like she just wanted confirmation of what she already suspected."

"I know Miss Jade," Tom said. He had not added to the conversation yet, but now both Taegan and Zorvut swung their heads to look at him. "She likes knowing people's business, but she also knows when to keep her mouth shut. I'd bet money she has more than a few other people's secrets that she'll take to the grave. I don't think the, ah, gravity of the situation would be lost on her in this case. Avoid her if you think that's best, of course, but I think the risk of her spreading any rumors is rather low." For a long moment, all three were silent, considering. Taegan's eyes flickered nervously between Tom and Zorvut, whose end of the bond was still muffled and distant. "Well," Zorvut sighed, leaning further back in his chair. "I trust your judgment. Both of you. Since one of us will have to go back to pay another week for the horses, I can't say don't go back at all, but... Do what you think is best for us to stay safe."

"Always," Taegan said, nodding. He managed a faint smile, then looked down at the table contritely. "I truly am sorry."

"It sounds like what you both need are a you can stick to," Tom interjected with a chuckle, shaking his head as the tension seemed to have finally broken. "Let's workshop some stage names, then?"

Chapter Eight

It was in his best interest to keep a low profile, so Taegan did not go out much for the next few days. The three of them soon settled into some semblance of a routine; they would typically have breakfast together, then Zorvut and Tomlin would walk out to the small backyard to train, leaving Taegan to his own devices for the rest of the day until they reconvened for supper. He tried to sit and watch the way he had the first afternoon, but while Zorvut seemed quite pleased with the progress he was making, to Taegan it all looked excruciatingly dull. To his untrained eye, they spent most of the day simply performing the same movements over and over again, and talking in strange abstractions like "seizing power from within" or twisting flame into thunder or squeezing it into ice. It all may as well have been another language entirely for how little he understood it.

Watching Zorvut train made him miss his own archery practice, but there wasn't anywhere in town he could safely use his bow, and he was not confident enough in their safety to go far from their home base, where their bond would not extend to. So he organized and tidied their belongings, re-read the two books he had brought with him, and puttered about the house, reading whatever else he could find on the shelves. It had been a long time since he had been so well and truly bored.

By then, it had been two days since he'd sent off his letter and had his unsettling encounter with Miss Jade, and it seemed to him that leaving for a walk along the beach would be safe enough. So he poked his head through the backdoor to tell Zorvut where he was going and set out.

It was a pleasant, breezy day, as every day in Naimere had been so far. A few streaky clouds dotted the sky, but it was mostly an unbroken, pristine blue, and as he approached the harbor, the line of the ocean on the horizon was a similar, darker shade of cerulean. It was picturesque—he tried to commit the image to his memory, knowing he was unlikely to see anything quite like it elsewhere. Aefraya had only a small border with the sea, its most northeastern point where the land dropped off in sharp craggy cliffs and the waves crashed below. It was a stark contrast to the calm wind and sand of the coastal town here, and he doubted he would ever return to Naimere again. After all, elven kings were not exactly known for being world travelers.

He moved a little further away from the noise and commotion of the docks, toward the quieter part of the beach where a few people were relaxing and swimming, though still a safe distance from them all. Carefully, he removed his shoes and took a few steps toward the waves. When the water lapped up to his ankles, it sent an icy shiver up the backs of his legs, but it was bracing—refreshing, even. Glancing over at the more populated section of the beach, he watched a child leaping into the waves, while her mother looked on in amusement and occasionally called out with encouragement. If it was suitable for a child to swim in, surely he too could give it a try.

The men he could see in the water were shirtless, so he returned to the sand, meticulously removed and folded his light linen tunic, and placed it gingerly atop his shoes. Then he turned back to the water and took a few more steps into it until the spray came up to his knees.

"Ah!" he exclaimed as an errant wave reached all the way up to his waist, smacking his bare belly with a cold shock. It left his trousers wet and clinging to his frame, making the cool breeze even colder on his damp skin, so he went a little further in, sucking in a sharp breath as the water came up first to his groin, then his hips, then his abs, and finally his chest. Though the water felt frigid upon the first contact, it quickly faded as his body acclimated to the sudden change in temperature, and when he spotted a wave taller than his head surging upward, he closed his eyes and let it fold over him.

Even though it had not been a particularly large wave, it still sent him tumbling backwards before he resurfaced, wiping the cold saltwater off his face and pushing back his drenched hair. But despite himself, he was laughing as he opened his eyes and swam out a bit further, finally getting deep enough that he could not feel the sand with his feet.

Though he had learned to swim as a child, it had only ever been in calm lakes for recreation, or wading through rivers that were never higher than waist-deep. The sensation of being tossed about by the waves as he swam was new and unusual; the movement was relatively gentle but still had enough strength to move him with the whims of the ocean, pushing him back toward the coastline despite his efforts to swim further from it.

The physical exertion was exactly what he needed, he thought when he finally relented to the force of nature and allowed himself to be carried back to shore. Even with his efforts to swim against the tide, it had brought him much closer to the craggy rocks near the harbor, so when he emerged cold and dripping from the surf, his belongings were a dark dot amidst the pale sand in the distance.

He trudged along the beach, tramping through the sand that stuck to his feet and shins, and by the time he reached his folded-up shirt he was mostly dry save for his dripping hair and damp trousers. But rather than get dressed, he sat down and looked out at the horizon for a while, trying not to think about anything, instead focusing only on the rhythmic motion of the waves and the constant, meditative sound.

Eventually, he started making his way back toward the street, buttoning his tunic as he went and walking barefoot along the paved path with his shoes in one hand. The sand that still stuck to his feet and legs dusted off with the movement, though he was sure he still looked fresh from the beach by the time he arrived back at Tomlin's home, smacking his shoes against the facade to shake off the last of the sand clinging to them before entering.

"Beach day, eh?" Tom called to him when he stepped through the door. The pair were sitting in the kitchen, Zorvut peering over his shoulder to look at him. "What did you think? Lovely, isn't it?"

"Very pleasant," Taegan agreed, chuckling. "Though I may have gotten a bit too much sun. Zorvut, perhaps you'd like to join me next time? It could be a nice break."

Zorvut smiled faintly as he approached. "Maybe sometime. We've been busy, though. We were just taking a break. I've almost got a new skill down, but it's proving trickier than the lightning bolt so I'll have to keep working at it."

Taegan's smile faltered slightly at that. "Well, good. Some other time then."

"Maybe I can show you once I get it down. Getting lightning from fire has been fairly simple, but making it cold—creating ice, that's been much more difficult."

"And you think this is the practical application you were hoping for? To be able to fight with it?" Taegan asked abruptly, looking down at the shoes in his hands. He could feel Zorvut hesitate, uncertainty trickling through the bond for a long moment.

"I think so, yes," he replied slowly. "And maybe some other things as well."

"Most of the magic I know is more practical, myself," Tom added quickly, glancing between them. "But there are definite applications to combat, too. I've been showing Zorvut everything I know about combat magic, but he's making good progress figuring things out on his own."

"I'm glad to hear it," Taegan replied, looking toward the stairs. "Well, I think I'll go wash, get some of the salt out of my hair."

He started heading upstairs without waiting for a reply. He should have known better than to try to pull Zorvut from his studies, but the rejection still stung.

"What did you mean by that?" Zorvut asked him later that night. He had just arrived in their room, closing the door behind him but remaining barely a step inside. "What you said earlier."

"You'll have to be more specific," Taegan answered, glancing up from where he was sitting at the desk, rereading one of his books once again.

"You asked if it was the practical application of magic that I had wanted," he replied. "And you felt... I don't know. Strange."

"Truthfully?" Taegan said slowly, leaning back to look over at him. "I'm hoping you've learned everything you wanted to learn, so we can go home sooner."

"Home? Is that what this was about?" he asked, frowning. There was a flash of irritation that was quickly pulled away. "I've learned a lot, Taegan, but I still have much further to go. We've been here less than a week. We can't leave yet."

"Then when?"

His frustration seemed to take Zorvut by surprise, and he considered for a long moment before answering. "I don't know. Once I feel that there's nothing else I could learn from him."

"And when do you think that might be?" he pressed. Now that he had spoken it aloud, there was an urgency in his voice—like when he had first realized how homesick he was, it felt as if a floodgate had opened where he had not even known there was one.

"I don't know, Taegan," Zorvut repeated, and he looked aside. "I'm doing this for both of us. To protect us. You know that."

"Yes," he sighed, the words sticking him with guilt. "I know."

"I understand that you want to go home," Zorvut said, stepping closer to him. "But I can't promise when that will be."

He looked away, back down at his book, and kept his mounting frustration contained firmly in the center of his chest, pulling it as far from the bond as he could. "Okay."

Zorvut waited for a moment, as if expecting more, then sighed and wordlessly moved to the wardrobe where he pulled off his shirt and hung it up. He blew out the candle next to the bed and laid down, his feet sticking out from underneath the blanket and hanging over the edge of the mattress. Taegan stayed up reading for a while longer, but eventually silently went to bed as well.

The next few days were much of the same. There was some distance between them—Taegan could clearly feel Zorvut's frustration, but it did little to assuage his own. Tom seemed to sense their conflict, too; his smile in the morning was a bit more forced and plastered on than it had been in the previous days, though he didn't pry.

He ended up leaving the house shortly after breakfast most mornings, and not returning until supper. Mostly he walked around town, though he did enjoy going down to the beach in the heat of the afternoon to swim. There were only a few taverns in Naimere; the largest was certainly Miss Jade's, but there was a smaller tavern near the docks that was only a pub, without an inn. Sailors and dock workers who didn't want to walk further into town for food and drink on their breaks were its most frequent visitors. He did not particularly like this tavern, but the patrons were always interested in talking with him to share stories about their travels, and he rarely saw the same person twice, which was a relief. The proprietor was a quiet, older human man with a bald head and a short gray beard who watched the goings-on in the bar with an intensity that distinctly reminded Taegan of a bird of prey. Taegan was not even sure what his name was, but the man did not ask questions and the wine was decent, and for now, that was good enough.

A new routine developed: he would eat breakfast quietly, listening to conversation between Zorvut and Tom with rare interruptions, then go for his first walk, making a long circuit around the perimeter of the town. Then it would be getting toward the middle of the day, and he would swim in the ocean to cool off and exercise. Once he was sufficiently dry, he would walk to the tavern on the docks and have a drink and a light lunch. Sometimes he would leave soon after, but other times he would linger for a while, chatting with other tavern patrons or just sitting and watching idly as workers filtered in and out of the bar throughout the afternoon. Eventually, he would leave to take another walk, this one shorter as he circled through the town square, occasionally doing some shopping before heading back to the house. Luckily, there was a bookshop in the town square, so even though the selection was not nearly as expansive as he would have liked, he still had something new to read.

At the end of the week, he finally ventured back to Miss Jade's to pay for another week of boarding the horses.

"Pay ahead for two if you can," Zorvut said before he left. "Or more if they'll let you."

He was already in the doorframe, so Zorvut did not see his sour expression at the words. "I will," he called out behind him, but heard no response before the door closed.

He kept his usual morning routine of walking and swimming, but this time he walked to the center of town to find the inn afterward. The stable was behind the inn, facing away from the town square; there was a girl he did not recognize on duty, and she jumped up as he approached. She looked just as young as the other stable boys they'd encountered, though, with the awkwardness of a teen as she moved. He guessed she was thirteen or fourteen at the most. She was wearing trousers that she had clearly outgrown, an inch of her bare ankle showing between where the pants ended and her shoes began.

"Retrievin' your horses, sir?" she asked, seeming to recognize him—he supposed the stable workers had doubtless talked about the massive horse belonging to the unlikely pair of an elf and a half-orc visiting town.

"No," he replied, holding up a hand before she could dart inside. "I'd like to pay for another week of boarding."

"Oh, sure," she said, sounding a little relieved. Graksh't was probably twice her height, so he couldn't blame her for dreading the idea of saddling him. "Just one week?"

He hesitated. "Yes, just a week," he said with a nod.

"That's five silver pieces each, so one gold total," she said, and he tossed her a coin. "Thank you, sir."

"I would like to see my horse, though, if that's alright," he said, and she nodded, gesturing for him to enter as she moved back to the small table where she had been sitting and dropping the coin in a small lockbox.

The door swung open easily, and he stepped inside, quickly spotting Graksh't at the end of the stable. It was not especially large, with five stalls on each side so room enough for ten horses, maybe more if they could double up a few stalls. But with a cursory glance, he could see that there were just a few horses boarded at the time, with only half the stalls occupied. He stepped toward Graksh't and found Ember in the stall across from him.

When she saw him, she started whickering, tossing her head eagerly as he approached. He did not realize how hard he was grinning until he was up next to her, patting her nose as she tried to nuzzle his face.

"Sorry, girl," he whispered, running his fingers through her mane. It was not braided the way it had been when he'd left her here, though it looked like it had been recently brushed and cleaned. "It'll be a little while yet."

He could hear her stamping her hooves from the other side of the wooden door, and for a moment he considered taking her out of the stall and just... leaving. If he really wanted to go home, he could—he didn't need a chaperone, he was not a child. He could just *go*. The urge to leave was almost overwhelming.

He caught himself as his fingers toyed with the latch on the stall door. What was he thinking? Zorvut was his husband. They had made the decision to come here together. How cruel it would be to up and leave! He didn't deserve to be abandoned without a word, no matter how irritating Taegan found his single-minded focus. He would not be any less lonely on the road by himself. That he even had the thought was a weakness that sent a spark of shame burning in his cheeks, though he pulled it away from the bond before it could grow any further, not wanting Zorvut to feel his selfishness.

He would have to satisfy himself with patting Ember's face for now. After a few minutes of giving her attention, he heard Graksh't grumbling and stamping from behind him, so with a chagrined laugh he turned and scratched the black horse's face as well. The massive beast peered down at him with obvious recognition and allowed himself to be scratched along his neck before tossing his head and turning away, seemingly just as fickle as Taegan's own thoughts. He deserved that, he supposed.

As he left the stable, he slowed his pace, glancing at the wall of the tavern as he walked back out to the front of the building. It had been almost a week since he had last visited the Snoring Seagull, and he did like it better than the tavern on the dock, despite his uncomfortable encounter with Miss Jade. An occasional visit would be fine, he thought, and besides, if she was going to do anything with the information she had, it was already too late to prevent it. So what difference would it make if he visited or not?

With a resigned sigh, he stepped toward the doors and walked inside. It was just starting to get busy, being the middle of the day, so even though Miss Jade was behind the bar, she did not seem to notice him at first, and one of the other barmaids came and took his order instead.

"Just a glass of wine, please. Whatever's your best," he said to the barmaid. Buxom and youthful, she seemed like the exact archetype of a human barmaid with light hair pulled back in a bun and a crisp white tunic with simple lace along the edges, the first few buttons undone. She grinned at him, and he glanced away nervously. Was she just being friendly, or did she recognize him? Maybe this had been a mistake after all.

"Coming right up," she said, and went to take more orders from the other tables.

Miss Jade had been chatting with another patron at the other end of the bar, but when she finally pulled away, she seemed to notice Taegan for the first time, a wide grin spreading across her face as their eyes met. But she said nothing, instead reaching below the bar to pour some drinks.

Eventually, she made her way over to him, bottle of wine in hand.

"I thought I was never going to see you again," she said in a teasing tone, and Taegan pressed his lips into a tight smile.

"It's been a busy week," he answered simply, and she snorted.

"Sure, sure," she chuckled as she poured him a goblet. "No, I'm sorry I spooked you. I meant what I said, though. I'm good at keeping secrets."

"Oh, I'm sure," he replied, taking a long sip of the wine. It was much better than the wine at the other tavern. "Well, frankly, yes, I did want to stay away for a bit after our last conversation. But then I had the thought, what's the point? You already know, and staying away isn't going to keep you from telling someone else if you really wanted to. And the wine's much better here anyway, so maybe it's best to come back more often and buy your silence instead."

She laughed aloud at that, throwing her head back. "Ha! And they say elves don't have a sense of humor.

Well, my fine friend, if you've got coin to spare, I'm happy to get you as much of your fancy elven wine as you can drink. How about something to eat? Today's special is the steamed bass, if that sounds appealing to you."

He grimaced. "I think I'll just have the vegetable platter, please."

Maybe it was the alcohol, but he had a surprisingly easy conversation with her as he ate, and her more friendly demeanor this time assuaged whatever lingering concerns were still in the back of his head. With the lunch rush, they spoke only sporadically at first, but he had nowhere to be, so he lingered at the bar for a while. When the rush died down, she came to stand near him again, chatting as she cleaned.

"So how are you liking Naimere? I don't think you have any beaches like this where you're from," she asked with a wink, and he nodded.

"True," he said. "I am enjoying the ocean. It's quite… novel."

"Nothing like it in the world," she agreed. "I mean, I'm sure there are port cities like this all over the world, and I've seen more than a few of 'em, but Naimere is something special. I think it's because it still has a small-town feel. It's not dirty and smoggy the way a big port city like Vlissingstadt is. There's enough trade for people to live comfortably, but not so much that it's strangled out the life of the town, if that makes sense."

"I understand," Taegan said. "Elven cities typically disturb as little of the natural topography and flora as possible, so I know what you mean. There is something that happens when a city becomes so large that you can't see the traces of nature still in it. We strive to never let that happen to our own civilizations."

"That's admirable," Miss Jade sighed, leaning back with a faraway glance. "I'm happy to live out the rest of my days here, but sometimes I think there's still so much of the world I've never seen, and what a waste not to see it!"

"I don't think that's a waste. There's only so much that can be accomplished in one lifetime," Taegan said with a wry grin. "But I can tell you a bit about some of the elven tree-cities if you'd like. Those tend to be the places tourists prefer to go, partly because they are so unique but because they are very beautiful, too."

"I'd love to hear it," she said, and leaned closer to him, propping her head up with her elbows on the bar. He stifled a laugh at the girlish pose, but she grinned widely, knowing full well the juxtaposition of the youthful body language and her world-weary face.

He spent longer than he realized telling her about the old elven tree-cities in the southwest of Aefraya, eventually shifting to stories about the capital, the temple-tree, the ancient customs of elves that had led them from their treetop dwellings to the castle built of stone and wood. For all his hesitance about speaking with her, now that the floodgates were opened, his desperate longing to go home sent a deluge of words from his mouth. He hardly stopped talking about his home save for a few interjections and questions on her part, until he realized the first of the dinner guests were starting to trickle in and he jumped up with a start.

"Goodness, it's much later than I thought," he stammered, setting a handful of coins on the bar—he'd lost count of how many drinks she had served him at this point. "I should be going."

"Come back soon, dear," Miss Jade replied with another wink. "It's been so nice talking with you. You'll have to tell me more about all these elven cities next time you come by. Maybe you'll just convince me to go on one last trip to see them for myself."

Taegan hesitated as he rose up from the bar, partly for the wine hitting him all at once as he stood, and partly to consider her words. Despite himself, a slight smile spread across his face, and he nodded.

"I'll have to come back to tell you more, then," he agreed with a grin. She laughed and waved him away, and he stepped out into the town square and onto the main street with a smile still lingering on his lips.

Chapter Nine

Once he had gone the first time, it was easier for Taegan to go back to Miss Jade's inn. The Snoring Seagull was livelier, the wine was better, and she proved to be an excellent conversationalist; clearly she was smart as a whip, but so far she had proven to be more trustworthy than he had initially thought. His daily routine shifted to accommodate visiting her tavern in the afternoons after his morning stroll and swim, as he started taking his second walk to the town square after drying off at the beach, getting lunch at the inn to drink and loiter until closer to sundown when he would finally head home.

But the situation with Zorvut and Tom had changed little, if at all. Zorvut was so absorbed in his training that he hardly seemed to notice when Taegan returned most afternoons, and interactions between them were standoffish and awkward. He had started pulling most of his feelings away from the bond in frustration, though Zorvut seemed to either not notice or not care enough to bring it up. They spoke rarely as well—they would exchange a few words over breakfast some days, maybe over dinner when Taegan returned, but Zorvut was often so tired from the day's exertion that he would go right to bed once they had shared their evening meal.

It was just as well, Taegan supposed; if they were not talking, they were not fighting. And they were not really *fighting* at all. He could not even say that he was angry with Zorvut, just idle and irritated. But words could certainly start to boil over if they were exchanged, so perhaps it was best they were circling around each other.

It was not sustainable, but everything had been so pleasant when they were on the road together that Taegan was not especially concerned. Once they went home, things would be better, he was sure of it. But the more they trained, the more Taegan suspected it might take longer than he had initially hoped; as unassuming as Tomlin had appeared at first, it was obvious he had some significant magical ability of his own. Occasionally, the retired bard would play his lute or sing a song after dinner, and even Taegan, with his meager sense of the arcane, could notice the shift in the room when he played, the way the very air itself seemed to be drawn toward Tom's presence and arc in the direction his voice, his song.

Whatever magic he was most skilled with, he certainly channeled it through his music, so it was humbling to think that what he was teaching Zorvut, strong as it was, wasn't his forte. Though it was impressive, it was still disheartening to think their visit might take much longer than he had first imagined. Zorvut wanted to learn everything Tomlin could show him, and a man with that amount of skill surely could not teach everything he knew in just two or three weeks.

And he still had not gotten a message in return from his father, though he was quite certain it had been long enough that the courier should have delivered his letter by now. He had suspected he probably would not hear back, just for their safety, but it was still a concern always at the back of his head. Had the courier brought the letter to the right hands? Was his father safe? He had not heard anything remarkable in the rumors that had swirled around the tavern—some reports of elves losing border villages, or pushing back and reclaiming them from orc invaders, but nothing regarding the capital or the king. But no news was somehow worse than bad news in his idling thoughts, forced only to wonder with no confirmation either way.

Most of his thoughts he tried to keep to himself, but after a few drinks at the tavern, he would sometimes let a few things slip to Miss Jade.

"So he's here to learn magic from his father, and you're here to... what?" she asked when he had mentioned Zorvut's training. "Keep an eye on him? Make sure he doesn't defect to the orcs?"

"No, no, I'm not concerned about anything like that," he protested, shaking his head. "More just for... moral support, I suppose. We didn't want to be apart."

"Well, no wonder you're restless," she retorted. "What in the hells would he expect? He might be here to work, but he's asked you to go on an indefinite vacation to somewhere you've never been, with no plans to do anything!"

"When you put it that way..." he replied with a grimace. "We didn't exactly have a plan beyond getting here to see what we could find out. I think neither of us truly expected to be here for so long."

"Sure, sure," she said, though her expression was still one of mild condescension. "All I'm saying is you probably could've stayed safe at home and the outcome would have been the same. And maybe it would have lit a fire under him to speed things up, get home to you faster. Not that I don't appreciate your presence, of course, or your coin." She grinned cheekily at that, and he managed a slight smile in return as he took a long drink from his goblet of wine. He was starting to suspect the same.

"It is what it is," he sighed. "I'm already here, trying to make the best of it."

At that point, another customer distracted her, and it was getting close to sundown, so he dropped a few coins on the bar, waved goodbye, and left.

After that day, Miss Jade would ask him how Zorvut's training was progressing at some point during most of his visits, and he realized he did not really know. It must have been going well, he assumed, for Zorvut always seemed tired and drained at the end of the day, but Tom appeared pleased with his progress. The last he had seen was when he had mastered creating both fire and lightning, and had been working on creating ice. Hopefully he had accomplished that as well, though Taegan wasn't sure what the goal was beyond that.

"It was just so boring to watch," he sighed. "It sounds much more exciting than it actually is. There were a lot of breathing exercises and practicing stances. I don't know enough to really follow the magic parts of what they discussed."

"I'm surprised the elves couldn't teach him more," she remarked, raising her eyebrows. "You're the ones known for having the best grasp on magic, after all."

"I think it was just too different," Taegan said with a shrug. "I don't fully understand it. But Tomlin seemed able to explain things in a way he could understand,

and that's how he's learned so much so far. As long as it works, I suppose."

At that point, it had been nearly three weeks since they had first arrived in Naimere; he probably should know with a bit more certainty how well Zorvut was doing. As he walked home, he considered how to ask about it without sounding flippant, or worse, like he was trying to push Zorvut to leaving sooner. That certainly would not go down well.

Dinner was largely the same as usual, and when Zorvut returned from his bath later that night, Taegan stood from where he was sitting and reading, catching his attention.

"Before you go to sleep," he said quickly. "I wanted to ask you something."

Zorvut blinked in surprise, but sat down on the edge of the bed and gestured for him to speak. "Go on," he said.

"I realized I haven't kept up much with your training the past few days," he said, though that was an exaggeration. "I just wondered what you were working on now, how it was going."

There was a beat of silence, then Taegan was surprised to see Zorvut glance away with a stifled chuckle.

"It's funny you would ask me that now," he said, shaking his head. "I had something I needed to bring up to you as well. Tom has taught me much, certainly. But I've gotten a pretty good handle on most of the combat magic he knows, and there's not much more he can teach me. But he was telling me about a friend of his, a warlock, out in Vlissingstadt who he thinks can teach me a lot more. He specializes in combat magic. Tom was going to send him a message tomorrow to see if he would be willing to tutor me."

Whatever Taegan had been expecting, that was not it. He hesitated for a long moment before replying, trying to calm his suddenly pounding heart.

"Vlissingstadt is awfully far away," he finally settled on saying, keeping his tone as carefully neutral as he could. "I don't know if it's really safe for us to be traveling more than necessary these days."

"But I can protect us much better, too," he interjected. "I know you haven't seen it yet, Taegan, but there's a lot I've accomplished since we've gotten here. I can set my sword on fire, throw bolts of lightning—there's nothing I couldn't protect us from."

"But that's still opening ourselves up to more risk, risks we don't need to take," he protested. It was getting harder to push down the panic tugging at the edges of his chest. "And how long do you think it would take us to get there? And how long would we stay?"

"It's about a week of travel," Zorvut said, looking away. Whatever he was feeling, he was keeping it closely guarded; Taegan couldn't get any sense of anything from him. "I'd anticipate us being there another three or four weeks like we've been here."

"Absolutely not!" Taegan exclaimed before he could even think about what to say. He bit his lip, forcing himself to choose his words before speaking again. "That would mean we'd spend over two months away from home. I can't be gone that long, not when we're still at war."

"It would benefit both of us," Zorvut said, still not meeting his gaze. "The stronger I am, the stronger we both are."

"I'm not going," Taegan said bitterly, crossing his arms over his chest. "If it means that much to you, go alone. I'm not leaving my father for that long."

Zorvut seemed to flinch at that, his expression faltering, and through the bond Taegan felt a faint flash of anger. "It's not like you've been here with me this far."

"Don't—" Taegan stammered, lifting a finger in accusation before biting down the words and clenching his hand into a fist, lowering it to his side. "I came here in support of you."

"And now you don't support me," the half-orc said flatly. His expression was carefully neutral once again, devoid of any emotion, and for a moment Taegan hated the cruel cast of his eyes, the hard line of his mouth, just different enough from his own that he could never get a good read on his face if Zorvut did not allow it.

"That's not true," he protested. "But my father, my nation—*our* nation—needs our support as well. There's only so much we can do from afar."

"Stop," Zorvut said, lifting a hand. "This isn't about them, this isn't about anyone but us. If you want to leave, I can't stop you. Fine. You left once already. I'll figure it out on my own."

All the anger flooded out of his veins all at once as his heart broke. "Is that really what you think this is about?" he asked hoarsely, his brows furrowing.

"I don't *know* what this is about," Zorvut replied, his face twisting the same way. "All I know is that you disappear all day and don't talk when you're here. You've broken our bond once, so what's stopping you from doing it again?"

"That's not fair!" he exclaimed. Tears burned at the corners of his eyes, but he willed himself not to cry, now of all times. "That's u*nreaso*nable and you know it. That was a completely different situation. I've been keeping myself busy because I have nothing to do here. I can't exactly help you with what you're doing, so I've tried to find things I *can* do to pass the time. You've seen me coming back from the beach—I walk, I swim, I drink. That's been my entire existence the whole time we've been here. I'm *trying* to stay sane, sitting here twiddling my thumbs while my father is at war. If you can't trust me on that, then that's an entirely different conversation."

Zorvut seemed to deflate at that, glancing away again with a guilty frown. "I just wish you would talk to me more about what's going on."

"There's been nothing to talk about," Taegan scowled. "I just told you everything that's been going on. Maybe you've been learning new things, but every day has been the same for me. It's boring, and lonely, so I've tried to keep it to myself to avoid distracting you. Zorvut, I... I really wanted to come here with you for you to learn as much as you could. But it's been hard to be so far from home, not knowing about... about anything."

For a long moment, Zorvut was silent as he looked out the window, unable to meet Taegan's gaze. He watched Zorvut anxiously, his heart pounding at each miniscule change in the half-orc's expression as he seemed to consider Taegan's words. After a long moment, he felt a faint trickle of emotion coming from the bond, then a jolt of something—a mix of frustration and guilt and fear and a tinge of melancholy. His end of the bond was no longer so carefully guarded, and Taegan could feel his conflicting emotions. Though in some ways it started to amplify his own worries, there was also a strange comfort in finally knowing for sure what the other man was feeling.

"I'm sorry," Zorvut said quietly, not quite meeting his gaze but looking down at his hands which were clasped in his lap. "I suppose I let my emotions cloud my judgment. You were having this hard of a time, and I didn't realize... I apologize."

"I understand," Taegan said, unsure what else to say. His hurt still lingered, but the anger he had initially felt at Zorvut's words had faded, burning out as quickly as it had flared up. "I'm sorry, too. I don't mean to make this about myself. We came here for you."

"Don't apologize for that," Zorvut said sharply, shaking his head as he finally looked back over at Taegan. "Just because we came here for me doesn't mean you don't get a say. I'll tell Tom not to ask that warlock, we won't go. I'll finish my training with him and then we can head back."

"I would appreciate that," Taegan said, and despite how his relief was tinged with guilt, he managed a tiny smile, which Zorvut hesitantly returned.

"I realize now that my training is probably not as exciting for you as it is for me," Zorvut said slowly. "Since you haven't had much to do, maybe we can set aside a bit of time in the evenings to spar? To help keep you a bit more active, and I can show you a bit of what I've learned, too."

Taegan chuckled. "I think that sounds pleasant. Although I still think you should come with me to the beach one of these days, too. It's very nice. Do you know how to swim?"

"A little, yes. You're right. Let's go tomorrow."

"Tomorrow?" he laughed. "I'm envious of how quickly you can change your mind. I might still be grumpy with you tomorrow."

"That's fine," Zorvut said, and held out his arms. "Come here." Slowly Taegan rose and stepped toward him, and Zorvut pulled him close, nestling his head against Taegan's shoulder. "I love you," he breathed, and Taegan wrapped his arms around the half-orc's neck, kissing the top of his head. "Truly, I really am sorry. I don't ever want to lose you... But that clouded my judgment."

"You won't lose me," Taegan said, shaking his head. "It'll be a lot harder than that to get rid of me."

"I'm glad to hear it," Zorvut said with a long sigh, the tension draining from his body. The close contact sent a warm rush of arousal through Taegan, but Zorvut shook his head, still pressed into his shoulder. "I'm sorry. I really am tired."

"Don't apologize. I understand," Taegan laughed. "Sorry to keep you up."

"Come lay with me," Zorvut said softly as he pulled away, laying back. Taegan crawled into bed with him, and although neither had blown out the candles, it seemed to take only a few minutes for Zorvut's breathing to slow into the steady rhythm of sleep. Taegan lay looking at the flickering candlelight for a long while before finally extricating himself from his husband's arms to blow out the lights and return to bed.

Even Tomlin seemed to notice their better mood the next morning as they ate breakfast. He was sitting on the opposite end of the kitchen, looking out the window as he strummed his lute and hummed a faint tune, but occasionally glanced over at them with a barely stifled smile. His relief at their less-tense interaction was nearly palpable. When Taegan met Zorvut's gaze over the cup of coffee he had brought to his lips, he could not help grinning as well at the look of recognition they shared.

"Tom, I was thinking we could end early today," Zorvut said after a moment. "I decided I should take Taegan up on his offer to visit the beach, so we'd like to go later this afternoon."

"That's fine, that's fine," the older man said, waving his hand dismissively. "You've learned just about everything, anyway. A half day or two won't do any harm." He winked at them from across the room as he strummed his lute again. "And Naimere's known for its harbor and the beaches, so it'd be a shame if you didn't spend some time down there while you can."

"I agree," Taegan said with a slight grin, and Zorvut only nodded in reply, although he too had an amused smile on his face.

He still went on his usual morning walk, but returned to Tomlin's home when he would normally go to the beach. It was as beautiful a day as all the others had been so far, with the sky clear and blue, no clouds blocking the sun from shining down on them. When he returned to the house, Zorvut and Tom were still working in the backyard, but when Zorvut noticed him, they seemed to quickly wrap up and he came back inside, finding Taegan packing a small lunch for them to take.

"I'm ready to go," he said, and Taegan grinned up at him. "Or should I bring anything with us?"

"We'll have lunch while we're there, so maybe a blanket to sit on?" he said, and Zorvut dutifully went to retrieve one. Soon they were heading out from the house, Taegan leading him down the street toward the harbor.

"Most people visiting the beach are on the north end of the harbor," Taegan explained as they walked. "So let's go to the south end, since it's usually less inhabited. It's more rocky on that side, so people don't like swimming on that end as much, but I don't think you'll mind."

"I trust your judgment," he replied simply with a nod. So when they arrived at the harbor, Taegan led them to the south end—just as he had explained, they could see some beachgoers in the distance on the north end, but the south side looked quite uninhabited from what he could tell. The harbor was bustling with activity, but they avoided most of it as they walked.

Taegan had not been on the south end of the harbor, so as they walked, it surprised him to see a smaller dock in the distance, which was hidden from view by the harbor from the other side. Zorvut pointed it out almost immediately after he noticed it.

"What's over there?" he asked, and Taegan shook his head.

"No idea," he said, and glanced back. "Want to go look? I don't see any ships. Maybe it's abandoned."

They made their way across the beach, clambering over rock formations and kicking up sand as they went. As they approached, Taegan's suspicions were proved correct—the structure was a tall pier that looked entirely abandoned, stretching out into the ocean several yards before crumbling into a mess of rotting wood far out into the surf. A set of wooden stairs still remained to attach the dock to the shore below, but even those appeared soft and unsteady.

"My guess is that this was a fishing pier," Taegan said. "And when the harbor got busier, it fell into disuse. Either all the fish were driven away or the fishing was just better from the new harbor than it was here."

"Probably not safe to get up onto," Zorvut remarked as they stood at the base of it. "It even smells like rotten wood."

"No, but it seems nice and isolated," Taegan said, glancing back at him. "If you wanted to...?"

Zorvut grinned, shaking his head incredulously at the jolt of arousal arcing through the bond. "Was this your plan all along?"

"No, but it's worked out well for me," he replied, setting down his basket of food. "Come here and pin me to one of these pillars."

"I can't say no to a prince," Zorvut said, carefully placing the blanket he was carrying onto the sand. Taegan was already walking out under the pier and pulling his shirt up, and Zorvut pressed him up against the wood pillar the moment it was off, pushing his hands down the elf's trousers and peeling them off easily.

"Don't let them get wet," he said breathlessly, and with a laugh Zorvut tossed them further up the beach next to their things, where the tide couldn't reach.

Their mouths crashed together and Zorvut's tongue pressed insistently against his lips. He opened his mouth to comply, and their tongues met in a wet, hot swirl of movement and force. The orc's muscular arms lifted him effortlessly, bracing him against the pillar so he could free one arm to unbutton his own trousers.

"Don't tease me," Taegan groaned as Zorvut's hands moved up his chest, brushing against his nipples and his abs. "It's been too long—please just fuck me."

"Ask me again," Zorvut growled, the sound sending a shiver up Taegan's spine.

"Please fuck me," he gasped, and he felt Zorvut nod against his shoulder. His weight was shifted to an easier position, and he wrapped his bare legs around Zorvut's waist as the familiar pressure of the half-orc's cock pressed against his entrance.

"*Fuck*," he whimpered as Zorvut entered him, setting a slow and leisurely pace that entirely betrayed the sense of urgency he felt. From where he was, he could see out onto the beach they had come from; though it was abandoned, there was no guarantee someone might not stumble upon them. The thought only sent an arc of heightened arousal through the bond, but whether it stemmed from him or from Zorvut, he couldn't tell. "Please, faster."

"No," Zorvut said, and Taegan stifled a moan against his broad shoulder. "No, I'll have my way with you. I don't care if anyone sees."

"No one can see us," he protested weakly, but he was completely at the half-orc's mercy. "You can't let anybody see."

"Let them see," he growled in Taegan's ear, moving unbearably slowly inside him. "Let them see you're mine. You're mine."

"I am yours," he agreed, and he couldn't form the words to protest any further. Pleasure buzzed through him, lighting every nerve ending in his body, heightened by the fear that wouldn't quell in the back of his head that at any moment they might be discovered. It was frightening and arousing all at once, and a tiny shred of him hoped for the thrill of being found out even as the rest of him screamed that it was unseemly, unbecoming, a terrible and dangerous possibility. His cock was trapped between them, the friction of the slow movement between them driving him to the edge before he could process what was happening. It was the hot, wet sensation suddenly pulsing between them that made him realize too late he was already coming, his mouth falling open in a stifled cry as his head tipped back.

"You like this," Zorvut gasped, moving a bit faster as the realization took him as well. "You want to be discovered. You want everyone to see us, to see me fucking you."

"No!" he exclaimed, shaking his head as his face burned red hot. But the evidence was undeniable between them, and he felt Zorvut chuckle. "No, that's not true—I—I don't!"

"Fuck, it's been too long," the half-orc groaned against him. "And you're so tight..." He could feel how desperately Zorvut wanted to keep fucking him long and slow, the iron will keeping him at the same slow and decadent pace, so he squeezed his legs tighter around Zorvut's waist, eliciting a long moan from him.

"Come *on*," Taegan urged, and bit down on the sensitive skin between his neck and shoulder. That seemed more than Zorvut could bear, and his hips stuttered and sped up. He was being well and truly fucked now, Zorvut's shallow movements setting a staccato beat that peaked with ecstasy at each rapid thrust.

"Fuck," Zorvut panted, unable to stop himself. "-*Fuck!*" He held out for only a moment longer, fire tearing through the bond as he came hard and fast. Taegan gasped and whimpered at the hot sensation of his belly being filled with come, his spent cock twitching weakly at the feedback loop of pleasure.

"Spoiled prince," Zorvut moaned against him when his hips finally stilled. "I wanted to fuck your tight little hole forever."

"Keep fucking me, then," Taegan replied, pressing his face into Zorvut's chest to hide his wicked smile as he clenched his muscles around Zorvut's cock, making him gasp.

"You just want to be found, don't you?" Zorvut chuckled, and Taegan could feel that for a moment he was considering it—then seemed to decide against it, slowly pulling his cock out. Taegan hissed at the sudden emptiness and the sensation of liquid spilling out of him in a thick gush that splattered at their feet. "If that's what you want, I'll have you again tonight. But I'd like to actually spend some time on the beach, not under it, after all."

"Who's the spoiled one here?" Taegan teased as Zorvut lowered him carefully. His legs trembled at first as he stood, streams of white come still dripping down them, but he walked further into the water where he could wash clean. Zorvut took a moment to watch him and finally pulled off his own shirt that Taegan had only managed to unbutton before following him, going out much further into the surf to fully submerge himself.

Taegan watched nervously as the half-orc disappeared under the water—he could not quite see him in the dark blue water, but Zorvut's head popped up only a moment later, grinning as he wiped the saltwater from his eyes.

"It's colder than I thought," he said as he waded up to where Taegan was standing—the water was waist-deep for him but went only partly up Zorvut's thighs, his softened cock on full display.

"Go put your clothes back on," Taegan laughed, and Zorvut only winked at him as he walked back up to where their belongings were on the sand. After he had scrubbed himself clean in the cold water, and spent a long, anxious moment looking out toward the harbor and hoping they had not been too loud, he stumbled back up to the shoreline where Zorvut was waiting and holding out his clothes.

It was a struggle to get dressed while he was still so damp, but soon they were sitting in the sun with their lunch spread out on the blanket between them, idly eating as they watched the surf.

"Thank you for inviting me," Zorvut said after a long moment of silence, tearing his gaze away from the horizon to meet Taegan's eyes. "You're right. It would have been a shame if we'd gone home before I'd been able to see this, to swim in it."

"I'm glad you decided to come with me," Taegan said, leaning closer to him as he took a bite of fruit, the juice dripping down his chin. "It's pleasant here, but it's much more pleasant with you."

With an amused smile, Zorvut lifted a thumb to wipe the juice from Taegan's face. "I love you."

"I love you," Taegan said, grinning up at him. They remained on the beach sitting quietly for a while after their meal was complete, then packed up and headed back home before the heat of the day became too intense.

Chapter Ten

Their afternoon at the beach felt like a weight lifted off Taegan's chest, and each day afterward passed by a little easier. Even though he went back to his usual routine the next day, something felt lighter about his usual walk and swim, and conversation with Miss Jade was lighter. The day after that, they sparred in the afternoon; while Zorvut was indisputably the better of the two in close combat, he was tired from his training earlier in the day so they were more evenly matched.

"Want to see what I can do now?" he asked with a smug grin after Taegan had won a match, smacking his shoulder with their blunt practice swords.

"Let's see it," he agreed, stepping back. They were in the alleyway behind Tomlin's home, still a bit narrow but with considerably more room than just the fenced-in backyard. Luckily, no one ever seemed to be in the area between the buildings, so they typically had the patio and the alley to themselves.

He watched as Zorvut took in a measured breath, pulling back his sword while making a gesture with his free hand like drawing a circle. A spark of flame glittered between his fingers, but the fire that erupted from it coursed up the length of his sword and flickered there, though it did not seem to consume the metal.

"Wow," Taegan said, instinctively taking a step back. It was an impressive display and more than a bit intimidating, though he knew Zorvut would never strike him with the burning blade. But if he were to see such a thing on a real battlefield, he would certainly think twice before taking on such a warrior—the intimidation factor alone was worth the effort, even if it had little effect on his actual fighting ability.

"I would show you my lightning spear, but I don't like doing it here," he said, and glancing at his sword, extinguished the flame. "It's harder to control. I'm always worried I'm going to strike one of these buildings, or someone is going to wonder why they're hearing thunder on a cloudless day."

"Understandable," Taegan laughed. "Still, Zorvut, that's very impressive. I'm proud of the progress you've made. When we left, lighting a torch was your best accomplishment, and now you can do this." He gestured at the sword, even though it was no longer lit. The sense of pride that welled up from the bond as he said it caused both of them smile almost shyly at each other.

"Let me show you this, too," he added, and he stepped closer to Taegan, gesturing for him to come nearer. They stood shoulder to shoulder, Zorvut leaning down to be more on eye level with Taegan, and he moved his hands in a swirling motion, brows furrowed in concentration. It took a moment for Taegan to see it—a few tiny snowflakes fluttering between Zorvut's hands.

"Ice is a bit trickier," Zorvut said, his eyes still focused on the space where he was creating the cold snow. "But I can also make it cover a... a larger distance. Damn!" The whirling snow suddenly faltered and fell from his grasp, most of it melting away before even hitting the ground.

"Still!" Taegan exclaimed, placing a hand on Zorvut's forearm. "That's incredible."

"Well, thank you," Zorvut said with a slight chuckle. "I'm just glad I was finally able to figure out how to make all this work. Now that I have some of these more basic techniques down, I'm hoping I can figure out more things that I can do just on my own."

"I believe in you," he replied firmly.

"Thank you, my love," Zorvut said, hugging him quickly before stepping away. "Let's go inside. It might not look like much effort from the outside, but I'm starved."

His lighter mood must have been visible, because Miss Jade even commented on it when he visited her next.

"Looks like you've worked things out," she said with a sly wink as she poured him his usual goblet of wine. He smirked in response, glancing away as he took the first sip.

"Yes," he agreed simply. "We've certainly, ah... cleared the air, if you will."

She snorted at that, not even trying to hide the grin on her face. "Say no more, sir. I don't need any details. I'm just glad you're not bringing your doom and gloom with you anymore."

"Doom and gloom?" he asked incredulously, raising an eyebrow. "That seems like quite an exaggeration."

"Don't try and argue with me about what's been going on in my very own tavern," she chided. "Now, what are you having for lunch?"

Once he had ordered his food, the place got a little more busy, and he didn't get much chance to speak with her at length. But a rather plain-looking human male sitting a few seats down on the bar kept glancing over at him—he did not recognize him as a usual patron, but unfamiliar faces were a common enough sight. It was hard to gauge his age, though Taegan would guess he was nearing his forties, with short reddish-brown hair and a slight sprinkle of stubble across his face, visible but certainly not a beard. He had seen the way men would look at him with desire or even just appreciation of his form, but this was not the expression on this man's face; if anything, he seemed almost curious, even surprised. Whatever that meant, Taegan was unsure, so he glanced away and tried not to make eye contact with the man as he ate.

But his disinterest apparently did not dissuade the man, who, after a few moments, pushed his drink closer to where Taegan was sitting and moved to a seat not directly next to him, but one over. Taegan glanced up as the man sat down, catching the human staring.

"...Hello," he said hesitantly, eyeing him. Now that he was a bit closer, he could see the man's clothes were plain but well-made, and the lines on his face were subtle but certainly there once he was up close. The man smiled at him, as hesitant as Taegan's voice had been.

"Hello," he said, his voice gravelly. His accent seemed different from the other humans in Naimere, but Taegan couldn't quite place it. "Sorry to bother you. It's just, it's rare I see elves in this part of Autreth, so I couldn't help but notice you. I'm a merchant, you see, and I do a lot of business in Aefraya. I'm in town for a while and was just surprised to see an elf here, of all places."

"Is that so?" Taegan asked, only mildly interested but trying to be polite. "What do you deal in?"

"I procure fine textiles from around the world," the man replied, the answer coming easily, as if he had spoken the exact words a thousand times before. "I'm sure you know, elves love their silks and flowy things, so it's always worth the trip. Although with things being as they are, maybe not so much these days."

"How long ago were you in Aefraya?" he asked. "It's, ah, been a while since I've been home."

"Oh, really?" the merchant replied, raising his eyebrows. "Well, you picked a good time to be away, then. I left just over a week ago now. Things have gotten a lot worse of late, so Aefraya's not a great place to be."

"Is that so?" Taegan asked, trying to sound as politely disinterested as possible to disguise the sudden anxiety that pierced him. His heart was suddenly pounding in his chest. How bad could the situation have become?

"Oh, yes," the man said. "If you've any family in Castle Aefraya, hopefully they took off in time. The orcs have besieged the capital and the castle. Rumor is the king has fled and is in hiding now, but who knows how much truth there is to that? All I know is I left Aefraya in a hurry and I don't aim to go back until all this blows over."

"The—*besieged?*" Taegan asked, now unable to mask the concern in his voice. "I—forgive me, this is the first I've heard of it."

"I was able to get out just in time myself," the man said, shaking his head incredulously. "Luckily, I just missed the invading force. I was on the road the day before they arrived at the city walls. That was about a week ago now."

For a long moment Taegan was silent, his mind racing. If the capital had been besieged for a week, it seemed unlikely his letter would have made it after all, or perhaps a mere day or two before it happened. If it had even arrived, would his father have received it? Where would he have gone? How had the orc forces gotten all the way to the capital so quickly, and in such numbers that the king may have fled rather than stand and fight?

"You all right?" the man asked, and looked suddenly sheepish. "Sorry, sir, I hate to be the bearer of bad news. I take it you had family in the capital, then?"

"I do," Taegan said faintly, unable to look at the human any longer. Suddenly all he could think about was getting out, getting home. "I—pardon me. Thank you for the news. I have to… I have to go." And without waiting to see if the man answered, he set down his drink and hurried out of the tavern, forcing himself not to break into a sprint, even though everything in him was screaming to run.

His resolve didn't last long, though, and by the time he was just outside the town square, he had started to jog, coming up on the house rapidly. He did not remember getting inside, but he must have slammed the door open as he did because he heard Zorvut calling out to him before he saw him.

"Taegan? Is that you?"

He stumbled to the back door where Zorvut was already coming inside, his brow furrowed in worry. His alarm must have been loud and clear through the bond, and even Tom looked concerned.

"What's wrong?" Zorvut asked, and before he could even speak, Taegan burst into tears, pressing his face into his husband's chest. "What's happened?"

"My father," he managed to gasp between sobs, shaking his head. "I was speaking with—I don't know, someone at the tavern, and—he said he'd come from Aefraya, a merchant, and the capital is under siege. They don't know where the king is, he said they think he might have fled, gone into hiding."

For a moment he could feel a spike of fear from Zorvut's end of the bond mirroring his own, but it was quickly stifled as the half-orc embraced him, squeezing him tightly in reassurance.

"Okay," Zorvut said, barely above a whisper, though the words still rumbled through his chest. His tone was measured and controlled as he was clearly considering what to do. "Okay. And you're sure? This man, he was sure?"

"Yes," Taegan said, nodding and wiping his eyes. He had to keep it together, he told himself, he had to hold himself together long enough to make a decision. "Yes, he was certain. He said, he hoped I didn't have family in the capital, that things went south just after he left. So it's been about a week, maybe two. Gods, Zorvut, what if—they could have—" The words stuck in his throat and he couldn't speak, but Zorvut squeezed him harder in understanding and he could feel him nodding as he spoke.

"I doubt it," he said slowly. "If they think he's gone into hiding, or if they're not certain... No, if Hrul had gotten ahold of the king, he would have made sure everyone knew it."

"We have to go back," Taegan urged, pulling away to look up at Zorvut. Tears blurred his vision, but he met the half-orc's gaze as steadily as he could. "We have to go."

He could feel Zorvut hesitate, could almost hear him protest—*How can we get back to the capital if it's under siege? What could we even do to help if we don't know where the king is?* but he did not speak for a long moment, instead taking a few deep, measured breaths. Though he could practically feel the gears turning in his mind, he had no idea what Zorvut was thinking.

"We'll go," he finally said, giving a tiny, almost imperceptible nod. His mouth was pressed in a hard line around his tusks, but Taegan could feel nothing from his end of the bond. Whatever he was feeling, he was keeping it tightly wrapped. "We'll take the night to pack and head out tomorrow morning. Tom…" He released Taegan to turn back to face him—Taegan had all but forgotten the presence of the human, who was leaning against the doorframe with a hand covering his mouth.

"No, I completely understand," he said before Zorvut could continue, lifting his other hand to stop him. "That's… a lot. That's a big deal. Of course you would want to go."

"Thank you so much for everything you've done for me, for us," Zorvut continued, his voice finally wavering. "You've opened your home to us and taught me far more than I ever dreamed possible. I can never repay you."

"Oh, please," Tom replied with a slight grin, though he too sounded suddenly heartbroken as he said it. "I'm just glad I got to know you. And, well, now that I know my son is a prince, I'm sure you can repay me at some point." He winked, but the smile on his face dropped immediately as he stepped toward them. "Do you need any help packing? Do you have the supplies you'll need for the trip?"

"Packing will be quick, I think," Zorvut said, glancing upward toward the stairs. "We don't have any rations for the road, though. We hadn't anticipated having to leave so soon..."

"I can handle that," Tom said, striding for the door as he said it. "What else do you need? Food, camping gear...?"

"Just food," Taegan said, wiping his eyes. The flurry of action helped dull the sharp pain in his chest. "We should still have all our other supplies."

"Got it," Tom called, already halfway out the door. They watched him leave, then Zorvut turned to face him.

"Let's go pack up," he said, then reached out to squeeze Taegan's hand. "We'll be alright. I promise."

Taegan's throat tightened up again at that, so he simply nodded in response and allowed himself to be led up the stairs. He could only hope that would be the truth.

Packing their belongings gave him something to focus on, yet it still seemed to go by in a blur. Somehow, clothes were folded and placed in their rucksacks, but he could not remember handling anything. Zorvut inspected the camping gear that had been stored downstairs, checked everything and set it by the door, and walked around the house to retrieve any of their belongings that might have ended up outside of their room. He was quiet and outwardly calm, but every so often Taegan would feel a flash of worry through the bond that was quickly stifled. Though he knew Zorvut was masking his feelings for Taegan's sake, it was strangely comforting to know the half-orc was feeling as wildly afraid and unsure as he was.

When Tom returned about an hour later, he was carrying a large canvas bag stuffed to the brim with food. "Got your supplies," he called from downstairs. "I'll put it here by your other things." A few moments later, Taegan could hear him coming up the stairs.

"Need any help with anything?" the human asked. Taegan was sitting on the floor with the last of Zorvut's clothes in his hands, folding them and placing them in a neat pile. "Wow, you made quick work of it."

"Yes, I think we've gotten just about everything already," he said, glancing around the room. "Just the bedding for tonight and clothes for tomorrow... Everything else has been mostly packed up. I'm glad I washed our clothes yesterday, so it's all clean."

Tom sighed, rapping his knuckles against the doorframe in a visibly nervous gesture. "I'm sorry to see you go so soon," he said finally, not quite meeting Taegan's gaze. "I, um... Well, I know we didn't really get to know each other very well, but Zorvut always spoke very highly of you. Maybe next time you and I can learn a bit more about each other."

Taegan watched him as he spoke with furrowed brows, but when the human glanced over at him, he pressed his lips into a smile. While it was not exactly an opportune moment to hear the sentimental words, he thought, the kindness behind them was unmistakable.

"Thank you," he said slowly. "Yes, next time, certainly. We really do appreciate your hospitality."

Tom only nodded in response, seemingly at a loss for words. Finally, with a sigh, he stepped back. "I'm, ah... I'm going to go see if Zorvut needs any help."

With that, he was gone. Taegan looked back down at the clothes in his hands before glancing around the room. Much as he had wanted to go home, this was not the situation he had hoped for, and he thought he might even miss their little room by the sea. But the very idea of missing what they had here filled him with guilt. He had gotten his wish after all, he thought, but the bitterness of it made it feel like ashes in his mouth.

Chapter Eleven

They planned to leave at dawn, but Taegan found sleep would not come. He laid awake for most of the night, looking out the window to the partially obscured midnight sky. He could feel Zorvut's waking mind thinking, also kept from sleeping with anxious energy, but neither spoke to the other. What could be said that would soothe either of them? All he could do was count down the minutes until they could finally set out.

When the first rays of sunrise started spreading across the horizon, Taegan sat up, hardly feeling the weariness in his eyes. He padded to the bathroom to wash his face and gather the last of his toiletries, and when he returned Zorvut was sitting up in bed with a pensive expression. They exchanged a knowing look that neither of them had slept, and packed the rest of their things in tense silence before heading downstairs for the final time.

Tom was also awake, though clearly much more sleepy, and was making a pot of coffee in the kitchen as they descended.

"A bit of breakfast for you," he said with a yawn, gesturing to the table where a few slices of toasted bread, butter, and jam were set out. "Coffee's ready in just a minute."

Taegan hesitated, glancing at the door where their bags were placed, but Zorvut raised a calming hand to him. *Wait* came through the bond, and begrudgingly Taegan nodded. They sat down for the light meal, though he tasted nothing as he ate, taking only a few bites of a single slice of bread. When Tom set a mug of coffee in front of each of them along with a small pitcher of cream, he managed only a few tiny, polite sips before the trembling of his hands made him set down the cup.

"Thank you again for everything," Zorvut said softly as they finally stood to leave. "I'll be in touch as soon as I can. Hopefully couriers will still be able to get through."

Taegan nodded wordlessly.

"I'll keep an eye out," Tom said, then opened his arms to hug Zorvut tightly. They embraced for a long moment, and when they finally pulled away Taegan could see the human's eyes glimmering with unshed tears. "Please, stay safe."

"We will," Zorvut said with a firm nod. Tom looked over at Taegan and offered him a hug as well—Taegan returned the embrace lightly, but pulled away after only a moment.

"Thank you," was all he managed to say, but the human nodded in understanding.

"Ready?" Zorvut asked, gesturing toward the door. They gathered up their belongings, Zorvut slinging most of the bags over his shoulders, then Tomlin held the door open for them and they stepped outside.

"Goodbye," the human called out as they left. Zorvut turned and waved to him, but now that they were out in the street all Taegan could focus on was getting to their horses and leaving town. His fingertips buzzed with the anxious energy, and though he usually had to jog to keep up with Zorvut's longer stride, they were now evenly matched as he hurried along the cobblestone road.

Though it was still quite early, they passed a few sailors and fishermen on the street heading in the opposite direction, toward the harbor. A few looked at them curiously, and one even turned around to walk backward as they went by to stare at Zorvut for a long moment, but eventually they made their way to the tavern unhindered. A stable boy was sitting sleepily in front of the stable, but startled awake as they approached.

"Closing out?" he asked, eyeing their bags. "You're the ones with the big ol' stallion, right? I think you have a few more days left you paid for—"

"No need," Taegan said quickly, raising a hand to interrupt. "Keep the change. We'd just like to saddle them and go, please."

"Oh—of course," the boy stammered, clearly taken by surprise, but jogged to follow them into the stable and help saddle the horses. He could not quite reach high enough to help prepare Graksh't, but brought all their gear and passed over saddlebags as they got everything together quickly. Ember whickered and stamped excitedly as they saddled her, but soon seemed to sense Taegan's anxiety and stilled, her eyes glancing about and watching each movement he made with concern.

Though he could not seem to leave fast enough, they were eventually mounting their horses and trotting out of the stable.

"We have to pace ourselves," Zorvut said softly, and Taegan gave a terse nod. As much as he knew it, it was still a struggle to keep from kicking the horse into a full gallop.

They had not discussed what, exactly, they could do when they finally made it back to Aefraya, and the thought of it rattled around in his head as they trotted through the cobblestone streets and out of the city gate.

If the king were truly in hiding, it was unlikely they would be able to find him either.

Their best bet, he considered, would be to stop at one of the land baron's estates before getting too close to the capital, to seek refuge and whatever information they might have to offer. They would pass a few on their way northward, though none directly on the path they would take, and he was unsure which of them might know the king's whereabouts, if any. They would pass several farms, but all would be on land owned by a baron, so there was no point in stopping at a farm only to be told to speak with the landowner. If his memory served, there were three large parcels of land owned by noble families along the way that were sufficiently far from the capital that Taegan did not think they too would be under siege, but were still close enough that they might reasonably have some idea of what was going on and could give them helpful information.

He mulled over his thoughts for most of the day, afraid to speak them aloud—as if putting them into words would give them a kind of finality that felt unbearable in the moment. Everything still felt like a bad dream, but forming a plan would cement the situation in reality.

He did not want to stop for lunch, but Zorvut convinced him to get off the horse for at least a little while so they could all rest.

"What have you been thinking about?" Zorvut asked him as they sat on a log a bit of the way off the road, sharing a loaf of bread and a handful of dried meats. Though it was all tasteless in his mouth, Taegan dutifully ate the portion Zorvut handed him. Clearly the half-orc had been sensing his turmoil.

"Nothing," he said faintly, shaking his head, and took another bite of bread. Zorvut looked at him for a long time with an unreadable expression, but did not press the issue. They ate the rest of their lunch in silence, and were back on the road soon afterward.

By the time the sun was going down and they were looking out for a place to camp amidst the wet marshy lagoon, Taegan's thoughts were clearer and he had a better idea of what they should do. Finding a dry spot was tricky, but eventually they set their tent up, tethering the horses to a small wiry tree to graze.

Zorvut still seemed tense, but when Taegan spoke as they sat in front of the fire and ate dinner, some of that tension visibly drained from him.

"I've been thinking about what we should do when we cross the border," Taegan said unprompted, staring into the flames. His emotional stability still felt tenuous, and he knew if he looked at Zorvut as he spoke he very well may start to cry again, which was the last thing he wanted. "Obviously the mountain pass isn't heavily guarded, so that is still our best bet. Once we're in Aefraya, I'm not sure how close to the capital we'll be able to get, but if memory serves, we'll pass by three estates owned by land barons. I think checking in with them will be the best option. They're far enough out of the way it's unlikely they've been affected by a siege, but they're likely to give us a better idea of what might be going on if nothing else." He wanted to add that maybe they would know where his father was, if he was indeed in hiding, but could not bring himself to say it.

"That sounds like a good plan," Zorvut said softly. "I'll follow your lead on this. You have a better grasp of all this than I do."

"Yet I have no idea what I'm doing," he said with a sharp bark of a laugh, but the bitter words faded quickly to the same nervous silence that had hung between them since the morning.

"No one would know what they're doing with something like this," Zorvut murmured after a beat, reaching over to gently squeeze Taegan's hand. "We'll take it day by day and go from there. The only way out is through, but nothing is set in stone. Let's plan on that for now, but we'll keep an eye out on the road for any news, all right?"

"All right," Taegan answered with a nod, still unable to look away from the flickering campfire. Staring directly at it was hurting his eyes, but something inside him couldn't bear to turn away.

He was certain he would be in for another sleepless night, but when their bedrolls were set out and he laid down, the weariness of the road and his lack of sleep the previous night seemed to catch up with him all at once, and he felt almost dizzy with exhaustion when he closed his eyes. Faintly he could feel Zorvut's hand on his back rubbing small, comforting circles, but soon that too was swallowed up in the relief of darkness.

Though he dreamed, it felt like fragmented thoughts, bits and pieces of events in a nonlinear order. He saw his father being cut down by massive greataxes, a bloodstained throne, a burning castle. But then his father was alive, searching for him with wide eyes, calling out for him as if he were a missing child yet when he tried to shout back, every muscle in his body froze in maddening silence. Hrul Bonebreaker stood over the crumpled, still body of Zorvut, laughing as he looked down at Taegan with a cruel glint in his eye. It was the vision of King Ruven laying deathly pale next to the mangled form of Taegan's other father, King-Consort Alain, each in a pool of blood, that finally forced Taegan awake with a stifled sob.

He pulled his blanket up to his mouth to quiet the wail that escaped him, and he felt Zorvut tense beside him, stirring awake.

"What's wrong?" Zorvut mumbled, reaching for him. Taegan could only shake his head for a long moment, gasping for breath. His whole body was damp with sweat.

"A dream," he finally stammered, but before he could speak again Zorvut's hand was clamping over his mouth.

Quiet! Came through the bond, as clearly as if Zorvut had said it aloud, and he looked to see Zorvut's golden-yellow eyes gleaming in the darkness, now wide-awake. And then he heard it—the stamping of footsteps, unable to be muffled in the muddy, wet landscape. He nodded in understanding, and Zorvut released him to reach for his sword. Taegan had not even realized it was in the tent with them, but Zorvut unsheathed it slowly and quietly before shifting into a crouching position and inching forward to peek through the tent flap.

Their tent was facing out toward the road, but as a twig snapped in the distance Taegan knew that whoever was approaching was coming from behind. Zorvut's head whirled around too, seemingly in recognition. Their eyes met, and from the bond Taegan had a sense of his bow, a quiver of arrows—he shook his head. He had been so consumed in his own thoughts, he had left his equipment with their horses, in Ember's saddlebags. Zorvut paused, then nodded once, held out his hand for Taegan to stay, and pushed the tent flap open all the way. Taegan lurched toward him, wanting desperately to follow, but he stayed put as Zorvut stepped outside and glanced around.

"Quickly," the half-orc whispered, leaning down. "Go get your bow."

Taegan stumbled to his feet and ran to the horses, barely glancing around as he went. But the sound of footsteps was closer now, and as he reached Ember and fumbled with the bag to pull out his bow and quiver, he heard Zorvut call out.

"Who's there?" he shouted, facing the darkness. The sound of footsteps briefly paused, then a voice called out in orcish, saying something Taegan couldn't understand. His heart dropped in fear—how could an orc party have made it so far past the border? And why?

Zorvut seemed to hesitate as well before shouting out again in orcish, then glanced back at Taegan and gestured for him to come closer. "Can you see them?" he asked, barely above a whisper. Taegan looked out into the night, eyes straining for any glimmer of light that might reveal who approached them and from where.

"No," he whispered, but then a faint movement caught his attention. There was a shimmer of something, like magic dropping away, much closer than he would have expected, and suddenly two glowing orbs of torchlight were visible about a hundred feet beyond their tent. In the flickering light, he could just make out two large, hulking forms—and between them, a smaller, slimmer shape.

"Don't come any closer," Zorvut called out, spotting them as well, but they continued walking. He held up his sword in a defensive stance, his mouth pulled back into a snarl. "I said don't move!"

"You know, we really don't have to fight," another voice called out, this time in elvish, sounding strangely familiar. Taegan frowned, glancing at Zorvut who was looking at him with an equally confused expression. But their moment of hesitance allowed the group to draw closer, and as they approached, Taegan could see the smaller form between the two orcs was a human. An older male, with short hair and some stubble—

Recognition sparked in his memory, and in shock he blurted out, "You're the human from the tavern!" His brow furrowed in confusion before the words had left his mouth. Who was this man? Why was he here?

A faint laugh answered him, and the three were now only twenty feet away if that.

"I am," the human responded, a slight smirk playing at his lips. "And I'm here to help, Taegan."

The man's form shimmered and almost seemed to melt off of him in the same way the surrounding darkness had melted just a moment before, and standing in his place was a taller figure, draped in a loose robe with long, dark hair and pointed ears.

Kelvhan grinned at him and extended his arms as if to display his handiwork.

Rage erupted from the bond, and even as Zorvut growled audibly he glanced over at Taegan as if waiting to gauge his reaction. Taegan's mouth worked wordlessly for a drawn-out moment, and finally he stammered, "How long have you been following us?"

"That's no way to speak to your knight in shining armor," Kelvhan chided, folding his arms across his chest. "Well, I would say that, but I think we both know why I'm here."

"Why *are* you here?" Taegan called out, holding out a placating hand to Zorvut before he could speak. If they could just buy some time, maybe, he hoped, they could avoid coming to blows that seemed inevitable now.

"To take my revenge, of course," Kelvhan snapped, and took a step toward Taegan. In the light as he grew closer, his eyes were open wide, a cruel grin on his face. Kelvhan had always had a stern, austere look to him, but something was different now—something absolutely manic in his eyes that made Taegan falter.

Before he could get further than a few steps, though, Zorvut lunged at him as his sword erupted in flame, illuminating them in a vivid light where there had been only dim torchlight an instant before.

"Stay away from him," he snarled, and for the first time a look of shock and genuine fear crossed the other elf's face. The two orcs moved towards him but hesitated uneasily as well, their eyes trained on the burning sword. But Kelvhan seemed to gather himself quickly, taking a quick step back and keeping his eyes on Zorvut even as Taegan drew his bow.

"I didn't realize you'd learned a new trick," Kelvhan murmured, seemingly more to himself than to them. "That's annoying. Oh, well." He snapped his fingers, and the two orcs behind him abandoned their hesitation as they rushed Zorvut with a bellow, both brandishing axes that glinted in the firelight.

Taegan loosed his arrow into one before his blow could land, and the other Zorvut parried easily before screwing his face in concentration—the air felt perfectly still for a split second, then there was a rush of heat even Taegan could feel as a thunderous bolt sprang forth between Zorvut's fingers, connecting with the other orc. The lightning was so radiant that for an instant the camp was illuminated bright as day, and Taegan turned his face to blink away the night-blindness.

"Good call," a voice said softly from behind him. Taegan whirled around, fingers fumbling with an arrow. But Kelvhan was already upon him, a wide grin on his face as he placed his hands on Taegan's shoulders, gripping them tightly and pulling him closer.

"Taegan!" Zorvut roared, turning away from the orc still slashing at him as the one struck by lightning s.

Panic overtook everything in Taegan's mind—he did not know what Kelvhan was doing, but a deep pit of fear had opened in his chest as the elf whispered an incantation, brows furrowed in concentration as he maintained a vice-like grip on his shoulders. Taegan dropped his bow and reached desperately for Zorvut—he could not break free on his own, but Zorvut was strong, if he could only reach him—

But it was too late. He could feel his fingertips just barely brush against Zorvut's before a lurching sensation wrenched him away and pinned him, motionless, in an inky expanse of nothing.

Chapter Twelve

He was dreaming, Taegan was sure. None of this could be real. He was dreaming, a bad dream, just as he had been before all this happened, and soon he would wake up to Zorvut next to him in the wilderness, sleeping and quiet. It all had to be a terrible nightmare.

For a long moment, he could not move and darkness surrounded him, though he had the distinct sense of falling. Then, finally, there was a different lurching sensation, like pulling back the reins of a galloping horse that bucked underneath him, and a dim firelight replaced the darkness, moonlight glinting off of metal into his eyes. Taegan winced, at last able to move, and raised his hand to shield his eyes from the sudden light.

It was cold, much colder than it had been in the lagoon where they were camping, and a breeze bit at his exposed face and hands. If he were not already shaking from adrenaline, he would be shivering with cold.

Kelvhan's hands were still clamped to his shoulders, he realized, but the pressure was soon relieved as the other elf released him with a bitter laugh.

"There," he said snidely, and Taegan could practically hear the smirk in his voice, though he was not facing him. "That wasn't so hard, was it?"

"Excellent, you've returned," a different voice called out, gruff and harsh—and familiar. Taegan whirled around, fear leaping into his throat, to find the huge figure of Hrul Bonebreaker behind them, a wide smile spread tight across his massive tusks. "Although, without my warriors, I see. I take it your little plan did not work out quite as you'd hoped."

Kelvhan scowled. "No, but I've brought you what you've asked."

"This is true," Hrul agreed, his eyes lingering on Taegan. Taegan looked away, eyes flickering across their surroundings for only an instant before realizing orcs surrounded them on all sides. They were standing in some kind of courtyard or perhaps a town square, encircled by simple wood buildings and elaborate tents. Wherever they were, he thought with a sinking feeling, was certainly quite far from where they had just been. He could feel his heart hammering in his chest, and tried to slow his breathing, which had become rapid and shallow without him even realizing.

The warlord said something in orcish, gesturing with one huge hand, and three orcs stepped toward them, drawing their weapons. Kelvhan took a nervous step away from them, getting closer to Taegan, but Taegan pushed him aside on reflex and the other elf stumbled.

"What are you doing?" he demanded, panic starting to rise in his voice as he looked back toward Hrul. "This wasn't—I just helped you! I did exactly as you asked. We had a deal!"

"Yes, but now you've outlived your usefulness," Hrul replied with a shrug, as nonchalantly as if they were discussing the weather. The three orcs lunged at Kelvhan before he could scramble away, two of them pinning his arms to his sides in anticipation of his magic.

"Taegan!" Kelvhan cried, eyes rolling in his head as he thrashed between them. "Please, please, help me! I'm sorry, Taegan, please!"

Taegan could only stare in panicked silence. The third orc, the one not pinning him down, raised a sword and drove it down effortlessly through Kelvhan's chest. The elf gasped wordlessly, the breath becoming a sickly gurgle drowned out by a gush of blood as the orc wrenched his sword back out, and Kelvhan fell dead to the ground with a wet thud.

Taegan did not realize he'd been taking a slow, fearful step backward until he felt a large hand on his back, pushing him toward the warlord. Hrul gestured toward the body and the two who had been pinning him just a moment ago lifted the limp form and carried it away, leaving a trail of blood behind as they moved. Then his eyes landed on Taegan, and a smile spread around his tusks once again.

"Prince Taegan Glynzeiros," he said, giving a slight mocking bow of his head. "Forgive me, I wasn't ignoring you. I welcome you to Drol Kuggradh. In fact, I have been trying to reach you for some time now."

He did not respond, waiting wordlessly for the warlord to continue. Even if he knew what to say, the fear in his throat would not have allowed him to speak. When the orc was met with silence, he laughed.

"You're right to be afraid," he continued. "Though I won't kill you, not yet. Let me tell you what's going to happen. Zorvut will be quite sure of where you are, certainly, and he will come here to free you. When he arrives, he will die, and then you will as well." He sighed, leaning back on his heels and folding his arms across his chest. "It's a shame, but his presence is the greatest threat to my victory against the elves. Some of my people still have some misguided sense of loyalty to that damned peace treaty and to him, even though he is not my son." He scowled at that, clearly vexed at the admission. "So, he must be taken care of, and so must you. Something tells me your death will break the king's resolve enough that we can take the capital for good."

Taegan looked around once more. There were at least ten orcs surrounding him, each of them armed. He had nothing but the clothes he wore. If he were to try to escape, he would certainly die. "And what makes you think Zorvut will know I'm here? What reason would he have to believe Kelvhan was working with you?" he asked, his voice hoarse. Hrul laughed at that.

"If he can't figure it out, he's far more a fool than I ever took him to be," he chuckled. "The warriors I sent with your elf friend should be more than enough of a clue."

He was right, Taegan thought, and the less the warlord knew about where they had been and what they were doing, the better. So he simply nodded once, looking away, and stayed silent.

"Nothing else to say?" Hrul prodded, but when Taegan did not reply, he shrugged. "That's fine. I have what I need." He barked out something harsh in orcish, and suddenly two figures were upon him, grabbing him by his arms and lifting him effortlessly off his feet.

"Wait!" he exclaimed, more out of fear than any planned protest. But Hrul glanced back over at him expectantly, and the two orcs holding him paused, so he had to say something, anything. "Whatever Kelvhan offered you, my father can double. Triple."

Hrul laughed again, but this time it was more of a howl as he threw his head back, his hands clutching his chest. "What he promised me was *you*. Little fool, I already have all I need. Go on, then."

The warlord waved his hand as if swatting away a fly, and Taegan was hauled off. He struggled against their powerful grips for only an instant before giving up, letting his feet trail limply along the ground as he was dragged between the two orcs.

Much as he tried to look around as they carried him through the streets, he could not glean much in the low light—only glimpses of wide dirt roads, dark wood structures, a handful of torches mounted on poles, and tents set up in the spaces between buildings. Eventually, they approached one of the wood buildings and pushed through the door, striding past another orc sitting at a wooden table who barely looked up to acknowledge their presence before he was hauled past, down a set of stone steps into a dark, even colder corridor. Only a single torch illuminated the gloomy hallway they were in, and in the dim light it took Taegan a moment to realize they were not in a corridor but a dungeon.

Unceremoniously, he was thrown into a cell, knocking the wind out of him as he landed facedown in the packed dirt floor. He lay there panting until the sound of an iron door closing behind him finally spurred him into action as he struggled to push himself up. By the time he stumbled back to his feet, the metal bars were locked shut and the two orcs were gone.

For a moment he wanted to scream, to beg, to demand his release. But he bit his lip and squeezed his eyes closed, forcing himself to remain silent—even if there was no one to hear it now, he would not stoop so low to beg and cry. When the fear boiling in his chest had calmed to a manageable simmer, he opened his eyes and looked around once more.

The cell he was in was fairly small, at least by orcish standards, maybe five or six paces across on either side, with metal bars on one end and stone walls on the other three, packed dirt beneath his feet. A pile of hay with a coarse gray blanket on top of it lay in one corner, and in the other, a low wooden stool and a wooden bucket filled with water. Nothing else was in the room besides him.

The only sound disturbing the stagnant air was his own shaky breathing, but after a moment, the silence in the back of his head sent him spiraling into another panic all over again. Zorvut's presence in his mind was gone, their bond completely mute. While it was not the sharp pain of their bond being severed, it was an uncomfortable nonexistence, evidence of a distance between them far beyond where the magic could reach. He was utterly alone.

Taegan pulled the stool into the middle of the room and sat down on it before his legs could give out beneath him, centering himself to the best of his ability. He was alone, and afraid, and cold—but he was alive. If nothing else, they had not killed him outright then and there. With every bit of elven stoicism and past training he could summon, he held onto that thought and tried to focus on nothing but the air moving in and out of his lungs. Taegan had no idea how long he sat there with his head in his hands breathing into the darkness, but eventually the impending sense of doom filling his mind began to gradually subside.

Exhaustion settled into him o his heart had slowed to a less-panicked rate and the adrenaline was no longer pounding through his veins, but the thought of trying to sleep now seemed as impossible as walking out the door. There was nothing he could do now, except wait.

Chapter Thirteen

A stunned silence fell over the camp when the two elves disappeared. Though he knew it existed and Tom had even mentioned such magic during his training, Zorvut had never witnessed anything like teleportation until now. Only an instant ago, Taegan had been standing there, reaching out for him, more terror on his delicate features than Zorvut had ever seen before, an animalistic fear screaming through the bond, begging for his help—and now he was gone, and the bond was silent. He had not saved him. There had been no sound, no light as they vanished. The only evidence that he had ever been there at all was his bow that he had dropped in the mud at his feet.

The quiet lasted only a beat, though, as rage quickly replaced his shock. With a roar, he turned back to the two orcs behind him, barely registering their uncertain expressions. Despite his effort at seizing the magic inside him, he could not summon another thunderbolt, instead filling his hand with flame that he hurled at the one further away, a male he had already struck who had an arrow sticking out of his shoulder. In a single fluid movement, he swung his burning sword at the closer orc, a woman, carving into her bicep. She howled in pain, but it was cut off as he swung again, coming around the other side to slice into her torso. The heat of the sword meant there was little blood, but the wet splatter of her intestines spilling from the wound was somehow worse. As she fell, Zorvut rushed the other orc, who was scrambling to lift his axe even as his clothes were still smoldering with the fire Zorvut had thrown.

The male orc got in one good swing, but it barely phased Zorvut—a flesh wound on his shoulder, something he could easily tend to later. Fear was evident on the orc's face, and his distraction was his downfall, for when his eyes flickered again back toward the place the two elves had stood, Zorvut plunged his sword through the orc's chest, cutting up through his ribs until the blade was buried to the hilt. The warrior's eyes met his, wide with shock, before rolling to the back of his skull as the larger form slumped forward lifelessly. Zorvut shoved him away, wrenching his sword from the warm body and releasing the thread of fire that had kept it alight.

Only then did he allow himself to look back at where Taegan had once stood, to stand over his ornate bow sullied by the dirt and water. He leaned down to gingerly pick it up, holding it in one shaking hand.

"Taegan!" he shouted, unable to stop himself. Fury still burned in his veins, but it was fading quickly to something colder. "Taegan! Where are you?"

He made a wide perimeter of the camp, shouting until his throat was raw. "Can you hear me? Taegan! Answer me!" But the silence, the nothing in the back of his head, was already the answer.

When he could shout no more, Zorvut sat down on the log they had set up in front of their campfire only hours before, looking into the cold ashes in a daze. He had to do something. He had to do *something*. He was called the Relentless; he did not give up. There had to be something, anything.

Whether it was the wound that he had left unattended or the dizzying panic that had finally set in, he found himself slumped on the ground as the first streaks of daylight were breaking through the night sky. He couldn't think long enough to formulate a plan. The only thing he could focus on was the emptiness in the back of his head, as if it were his tongue running over the raw empty space where a broken tooth had been yanked out.

Mechanically, without realizing until he was halfway done with the task, he started breaking down camp, carefully folding Taegan's bedding and setting it into his pack. It was so much smaller than his own. He would not cry. He could not cry, not now.

When everything was packed and piled onto Ember, Taegan's little dun mare, he strung a rope through her reins and leashed her to Graksh't before mounting the larger stallion. Though his hands were shaking, Graksh't seemed to know the way, following the trail without need of Zorvut's guidance.

There was nothing else he could do. It would be a long road to get home now.

When Zorvut arrived back in Aefraya, there was no siege. From the moment he could see it in the distance, the shape of the city streets spiraling up the hill with the castle perched at the top, his suspicions that Kelvhan had tricked them from the start proved true. Castle Aefraya looked just as idyllic as ever, the white stone gleaming in the afternoon sun. He did his best to push down the anger and sinking despair that welled in his chest at the realization, and made his way up to the city gates and through to the castle with as neutral an expression as he could manage.

"Tell the king I've returned," he said gruffly to the guard that met him at the gate. Though the guard hesitated—through the elf's helmet Zorvut could not see his face, but he was sure he was looking fearfully at the prince's lone horse—he nodded and jogged up toward the castle entrance. A stableboy was already running up to take their horses. Zorvut tossed him Graksh't's reins without looking, unable to bear the boy's nervous expression. He felt as if every guard standing between the gate and the castle was staring right at him, so he kept his gaze firmly on the ground as he slowly made his way up the steps and to the castle door.

As he stepped into the foyer, he could already hear hurried footsteps approaching from the marble staircase. He looked up to see the king, pulling a fine robe over his leisure clothes, descending the stairs quickly, followed closely by his attendant.

"Zorvut!" Ruven exclaimed. The half-smile on his face slowly dropped as he saw Zorvut was alone, recognizing the grim expression he couldn't hide. "Where is Taegan?"

He took in a long, steadying breath, looking back down at his feet. Already he could not bear the king's frightened visage.

"Captured," he said hoarsely, clearing his throat. He could not cry, not yet. "We were tricked, and he was taken. The elf who betrayed us, Kelvhan, he must have been working with orc forces. He had approached Taegan in disguise, as a merchant, and told him the capital was under siege, that you were in hiding or dead. And he was so worried that we left, and Kelvhan accosted us on the road, and..."

He trailed off, his voice breaking again. Ruven was silent, and he still could not bring himself to look up at the elf. Instead, he first knelt, then lowered his forehead to the ground, prostrating himself before the king.

"I am so sorry," he choked out over the lump in his throat. "King Ruven, I am so sorry. I couldn't save him. All this effort was in vain, because I couldn't—I couldn't keep him safe."

"Get up," the king's voice cut through sharply. "Zorvut. Please, get up."

Zorvut took in a few gasping breaths, willing himself not to break down, before pushing himself back up to his feet. When he looked up at the king, Ruven's face was pale, his expression stern, but his hands were steady as he gestured for Zorvut to rise.

"Come speak with me in my private study," he said, turning to go without waiting to see if Zorvut followed. Not that he could refuse an order from the king, so he silently followed him up the marble stairs and to his study.

The king's attendant closed the door behind them, leaving the two of them alone. King Ruven stood near the open window, looking down at the city with a pensive expression, before turning to face Zorvut again.

This time, his hands trembled, but he clasped them firmly in front of himself in a steadying gesture before speaking once more.

"Tell me everything that happened," he said in a low voice.

"Kelvhan had magically disguised himself as a trader, a—a merchant," Zorvut replied, fixing his gaze on the tall bookshelf behind Ruven rather than on the king's eyes burning with barely contained emotion. "He told Taegan that he had just fled Aefraya after orcs had taken the castle, and that the fate of the king was uncertain. Taegan was afraid for you, and wanted to leave immediately, so we did. But Kelvhan and two orcs ambushed us on the road that night, and he... I don't know. He grabbed Taegan and teleported him away. At least, I think so—I've never seen magic like that before."

"And the orcs with him?"

"No, I killed them. But I doubt they would have told me anything, even if I had let them live."

For a long minute, the king did not respond, looking back out through the window as he mulled over the information. When he spoke again, his voice was even and forceful, more so than Zorvut would have expected. "Did you learn everything you needed to, in Naimere?"

The question took Zorvut by surprise, and he was silent for a long moment before answering. "Yes, as much as he could teach me."

"Then this was not in vain," the king said with a surprising sternness, finally turning away and looking back toward him. "I believe you are correct that Kelvhan must be working with the warlord, though to what benefit I could not say. But Taegan is surely alive. Hrul Bonebreaker may be a violent man, but he is also a tactical thinker. He has to be to maintain control of his tribes. He would realize Taegan is of far more value to him alive than dead."

"Yes," Zorvut agreed, nodding once. At least, he certainly hoped that was true.

"You know the warlord better than I," Ruven continued. "Tell me. Do you think he is trying to bait you, or me?"

Zorvut considered it for a moment. "Me, I think. I would guess that… he underestimates your trust in me, and is hoping I will go straight for him without having alerted you, for fear of your wrath. If he had wanted to goad you, I think you would have already known he has Taegan."

"I think so, too," he agreed. "And if that is the case, we will play into his expectations for now. I will summon some of my generals back from the field to discuss this with them and come up with a plan. We must act quickly if he is expecting you to pursue him, but it's unlikely anything will be decided before tomorrow. Can I trust you to wait until then?"

When he looked over at the king, Ruven was watching him with an intense gaze. Though he had learned to read Taegan's face fairly well over time, the elven king with his cold, austere countenance remained wholly inscrutable to him.

"Yes," he said, swallowing hard. Much as he wanted to get back on his horse and ride straight for Drol Kuggradh, he knew that their next steps needed to be perfectly calculated. As the king had said, Hrul Bonebreaker was a tactician in his own right, and Zorvut could not outmaneuver him alone. He needed the elves. "You are the king. I follow your commands."

King Ruven's hard expression finally softened at that, and for the first time Zorvut caught the slight hint of despair in his face. "I am the king. But you are my son-in-law." He took a step toward Zorvut and placed a hand on his forearm. "And I know you love my son. I know he trusts you, and so I trust you as well." He paused, his mouth opening silently before pressing back together in a hard line as if he wanted to say more, but stopped himself.

"Thank you," Zorvut said faintly. His words were a relief to hear. Though he knew the king to be fair, he also knew how zealously he would protect Taegan—part of him would not have been surprised if Ruven meted out some punishment for his failure to save the prince, though perhaps that instinct resulted from the warlord, rather than the elven king.

"Get some rest," Ruven sighed before stepping back once more. "Tomorrow we will plan. It has been a long journey for you, I'm sure, so until then, rest while you can."

"I will," Zorvut said, and the door to the study opened behind him. He bowed his head before walking toward the door, but the king had already turned away again.

Taegan's attendant, Aerik, was not in the corridor when he arrived back at their quarters. But when he stepped inside, candles had been lit throughout the room—and even from the entryway, he could see that a warm bath had been drawn, and that was what finally broke him.

All that his spoiled, sweet prince had wanted was the comfort of a good bath and his own bed. From the start, he had so desperately yearned to come home. And now he was here, and Taegan was further away than ever before.

Zorvut threw his things to the floor and crawled into bed fully clothed, finally letting the tears come. Though their sheets had been laundered in their absence, they still had the faint scent of Taegan, the oil he used to smooth his hair and the rosewater he loved to bathe in. His mind kept pulling away to the point in the back of his skull where their bond sat, where he could always sense Taegan, his charm, his fire. But each time it was still empty, still silent.

Even as he wept, he knew what he had to do. He would never get his husband back unless the warlord was dead.

TO BE CONTINUED

About the Author

Lionel Hart (he/him) is an indie author of MM fantasy romance and paranormal romance. Currently, he resides in north San Diego with his husband and their dog. For personal updates and new releases, follow the links below.

Twitter: @lionelhart_

Facebook: Lionel Hart, Author

TikTok: @author.lionelhart

Email Newsletter

Also By Lionel Hart

Chronicles of the Veil
1. The Changeling Prophecy
2. The Drawn Arrow

The Orc Prince Trilogy
1. Claimed by the Orc Prince
2. Blood of the Orc Prince
3. Ascension of the Orc King

Heart of Dragons Duology
1. Beneath His Wings

Printed in Great Britain
by Amazon